Wealthy Puritan orph[...]
known affection. Broug[...]
ing aunt and uncle, and [...]
sake, she has had to lea[...]
duty—even agreeing t[...]
pleasant Sir Edward B[...]
ding. But Sir Edward has an enemy who strikes at him
by kidnapping Deborah and imprisoning her under the
threat of death—a daring Royalist highwayman, seeking ransom money for the exiled King Charles II's
cause. Yet, despite her terror, Deborah is to find more
happiness than she has ever known before as the prisoner of the notorious Captain Black....

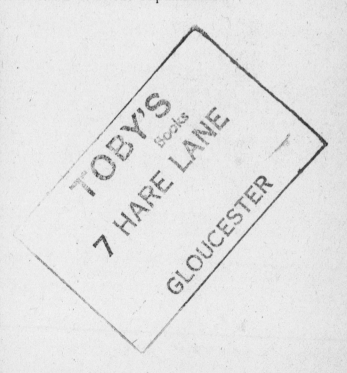

Captain Black
Caroline Martin

MILLS & BOON LIMITED
London · Sydney · Toronto

First published in Great Britain 1980
by Mills & Boon Limited,
15–16 Brook's Mews, London W1Y 1LF

© Caroline Martin 1980

Australian copyright 1980
Philippine copyright 1980

ISBN 0 263 73227 4

Set in Baskerville

Made and printed in Great Britain by
C. Nicholls & Company Ltd.,
The Philips Park Press, Manchester

CHAPTER
ONE

'Don't slouch over the table like that, girl. Straighten your back. You are a woman now, soon to be a wife. At least try to cultivate a semblance of dignity.'

'So many girls these days seem to think slovenly posture is a sign of modesty. Better to have true modesty and humility of heart, and a straight back, say I.'

'Yes indeed, my dear husband. And I'm afraid Deborah has a great way to go before she reaches that. Sometimes I think that inheritance has gone to her head. Did you see her crossing the hall just now before prayers, tripping along like any heedless wanton?'

An indignant clicking of the tongue.

'I think it a very bad thing for so young a girl to be encumbered with so much of this world's goods. It must lead her to think herself too good for those of us who have not her worldly advantages. That kind of vanity must be knocked out of her. If she cannot be poor indeed then she must at least learn to have true poverty of spirit. It is fortunate for Sir Edward that we have a few weeks to begin the moulding of her. Your sister seems to have sadly neglected her duties. There is nothing in her manner fitting to the outward adornment of a good and obedient wife.'

'I must agree with you there, husband. And these small outward signs are important as marks of grace within—a sober bearing is essential, not that undignified scampering about the place. And her appearance, too—no godly young maid should permit herself to traipse around with lovelocks hanging about her face, if she wants to keep her reputation....'

Deborah sat between the two of them, head meekly bent, the two voices from the table ends meeting over the neat plain whiteness of her cap from which the offending curls of her hair escaped despite all her efforts to control them.

'They talk about me just as if I weren't here—or as if I were deaf, or an idiot,' she thought, but with resignation.

Contrary to her uncle's assumption, her dead mother had in no sense neglected her duty. But for the slight difference of voice, the Kentish accent, she could have been listening to her mother speaking to her now—or her father.

She had long ago schooled herself not to be hurt or angered by the behaviour of the adults who had ruled her from childhood. If her spirit was not utterly broken after seventeen years of the rigid loveless discipline which was all she had ever known of parental care, then it was thanks to her own ability to accept the worst they could do to her with a patience and self-control which would not allow them anywhere near her essential self.

Now half-hearing these two, her uncle and her aunt, discussing her failings and weaknesses as coolly as if she were no more than a new mare in the stables, she did not intervene to defend herself, but let it pass her by as if it had nothing at all to do with her.

'In these uncertain times,' Aunt Susan went on, 'it is all the more important that those of us who are able to set an example by our behaviour should do so. Now that the Lord Protector Oliver is dead, and no one seems quite to know what will happen next, it is the more important that there should be firm principles to guide our lives.'

'Yes indeed,' agreed her husband. To Henry Foster, as to his wife and to Deborah's parents, Oliver Cromwell had been a hero, a giant among pygmies—and had without doubt somehow grown in stature since his death last year. Deborah prepared herself for a long and gloomy dissertation on the present disorders in the country: no settled government, and the army leaders contending for power. It was a favourite topic in this house.

'We need a strong man to take charge,' her uncle asserted as usual, but Deborah did not listen. There was no point in her doing so, for they would not have welcomed her involvement in their discussion. She was an uninformed and wayward girl, not permitted to hold opinions. So those she did hold, and they were few, she kept to herself.

She would have hated Cromwell's name, simply because it had always been held up to her as an example of the ideal Puritan; but for two things she knew of him from her days at home in London. When his daughter Frances had been married, it had been said by one of the servants out of Mistress Halsey's hearing, that Whitehall was ablaze with candles for the occasion, and there had been music and dancing and a scene such as might have graced the court of the dead King Charles. Deborah had not altogether believed it—after all, her parents had always thought dancing and any music but the psalms to be the playthings of the devil. And then, one day on her way home from church, she had seen the Lord Protector himself dismount from his carriage at a house close by, and with him his daughter Elizabeth. She had paused to watch, and seen the gentleness and concern and the transparent love which had marked the father's manner and expression towards his daughter. And she had gone on her way with a new sharp envy intensifying her inevitable loneliness. If only the human qualities of the Protector could have impressed her parents as much as his moral ones!

The simple breakfast had long been eaten, and still they sat on at table, Deborah silent between the two voices lugubriously discussing the nation's troubles. And then her uncle's steward interrupted them with deferential hesitancy, and Henry Foster took his leave of them. His wife, able now to give her undivided attention to her niece, subjected her to a long and sharply critical scrutiny.

'It may be that you are sound at heart, my child,' she said in a tone heavy with doubt, 'but there are over many corners still to be hammered away before we come to that, I fear. Still, you are young yet.' Her gaze was caught once again by the dark glossy tendrils of hair falling over Deborah's forehead. 'Did your mother never speak to you about your appearance?'

'Far too often,' thought Deborah. But all she said was: 'Yes, aunt.'

'It seems to have had little effect,' observed Susan Foster, tight-lipped. 'I had intended that you should come with me to the kitchens this morning. If your undignified manner of gossiping with Betty when we sorted the linen yesterday was anything to go by, I suspect your education in the duties of a housewife has been as neglected as everything else. Betty was there to do her duty as my servant, not to tell you all about her family troubles. You may learn something to your advantage if you see how I deal with the servants. But as you are at present I could not take you before them! You must go to your room and see what you can do to make your appearance more seemly. Then when you have presented yourself to me here, and I have approved what you have done, we shall go about our duties. Always remember, my child, that as mistress of a household (as you soon will be, God willing), your example must always be of the highest to those weaker vessels who serve under you. Lovelocks' what a depth of distaste she put into the word, Deborah thought 'are wholly unacceptable.'

'Yes, aunt,' said Deborah. Then, hastily, 'I mean, no, aunt.'

'I shall expect you very shortly. A woman whose mind is not on vain things does not take all day over her toilette.'

'No, aunt.'

Deborah dropped a dutiful curtsy, and made her way as quickly as she could without indulging in the hasty tripping pace which had evoked such disapproving comment at breakfast, across the hall and up the wide stairs to her room. As she went she wondered idly why, if the Lord had not meant women to spend too long in attending to such matters, He had given her this thick springy hair which even hours of labour could not keep within decent bounds for long.

In her room she found Nan, her maid, who had come with her from London, seated at the window mending the torn hem of a gown. Nan—one of those 'weaker vessels' to whom she must be careful to set a good example—was perhaps her only friend. She was certainly the only person she did not habitually address with fearful respect; and who did not treat her in return as if she were a wilful and disobedient child.

'Aunt Susan has sent me to tidy my hair,' Deborah explained in answer to Nan's questioning look. Nan grinned, and put her sewing aside.

'If the Good Lord had meant you to have tidy hair he'd not have made it curl so thickly,' she said, unconsciously echoing Deborah's rebellious thought of a moment ago. 'But there, some folks can't be told. Here, let me see what I can do.' She dragged a stool to the window, and Deborah sat on it while Nan pulled off the cap and struggled with the recalcitrant locks.

'I thought you'd be wanting that gown to go to

Sandwell tomorrow,' the servant went on. 'But it's a good thing I looked it out. I'd forgot you'd torn the hem last time you had it on.'

'Yes,' said Deborah, a little absently, her stomach tightening momentarily at the thought of tomorrow. She had been betrothed to Sir Edward Biddulph for some weeks now—it had been arranged very quickly, almost as soon as she had come here after her mother's death—but the bridegroom had been absent on business at the time, and it was not until tomorrow that she would see him. They had told her very little, except that he was, of course, a man of undoubted godliness and impeccable morals, and a bachelor, somewhat older than herself. She wished she could be sure that she had no reason to feel anxious about tomorrow.

With an effort she turned her thoughts to more immediate matters.

'I'm to be allowed in the kitchens this morning,' she said, 'so that Aunt Susan can show me how to behave towards the servants.'

Nan gave a splutteringly irreverent laugh. 'She and your mother—two of a kind, they are! Thank the Lord, they never did manage to teach you their way—and may that always be so, say I.'

'My mother was a most competent housewife—and so is Mistress Foster,' Deborah returned quietly. 'I expect I could learn a great deal, if I were more teachable. But I think I'm not a very apt pupil.'

'And you know why?' returned Nan. 'Because you can't bring yourself to treat everyone else as if they counted for nothing beside you. You think us all as much God's children as you are yourself. Maybe you won't have everything quite so neat and well-ordered in your house when you're wed, but it'll be a happier one for all that. And I'll hold to that to your aunt's face, if she should ask me. Which she won't—In any case, it's

my belief she's jealous of your wealth, and that's why
she's so harsh to you.'

'Oh no,' said Deborah quickly. 'She is only anxious
that it should not lead me astray. And it's quite right
that she should be concerned. After all, she doesn't
know how very little it all means to me. I can only be
grateful that she cares so much about me.'

Nan gave a sceptical snort.

'Think the best of her if you will, Mistress Deborah.
It's like you. But you'll not alter what I think.' She
paused, and stood back to survey her handiwork.
'There,' she said, 'now you're fit to appear before
kitchen wenches and like lowly persons.'

Mistress Foster did not allow the members of her
household the concession of a mirror; after all, it would
only have served to encourage vanity: so that Deborah
could not see how she looked. But she put up a hand to
reassure herself that every strand of her hair was now
ruthlessly confined within the cap.

'Thank you, Nan,' she said, and stood up. 'Now for
Aunt Susan.'

She left the room slowly, with growing reluctance. At
her window just now she had looked out on a world of
gold and bronze and blue, the trees gorgeous with
autumn colours under a brilliant sky, a scene which
seemed to offer her an escape from the restrictions and
repressions of life within these walls. But duty came
first: that she had learnt almost before she could talk,
from her father when she was a child, from her mother
as she grew older, from her aunt and uncle more
recently. Duty had taken her father to fight against the
enemies of the Parliament at Worcester, where he had
died at the moment of his party's victory; duty had
taken her mother, already ill, to the weekly prayer
meeting on the coldest night of the winter, and brought
on the raging fever which had killed her. Duty had

surrounded Deborah from infancy, the motivating
force of her upbringing, the principle which had guided
them all in moulding and disciplining the lonely child
until she had grown into the equally lonely young
woman who stood here now with her marriage and a
whole host of new duties before her. Lonely. Unloved.
But dutiful.

Suddenly, on an impulse stronger than any she had
known before, so strong that even her sense of duty was
not proof against it, Deborah rebelled.

It was not a very spectacular rebellion, and in anyone
else it would have seemed no more than a minor mis-
demeanour, rather childish perhaps; but for Deborah it
marked a new phase, a sudden violent assertion of her
long-suppressed independence. At the foot of the stairs
she did not make her way as she ought to have done to
the parlour where Mistress Foster waited, but turned
instead to the little half-concealed door under the stair-
case which led, enticingly, into the golden sunlit garden.

Outside, with the door closed firmly behind her,
Deborah stood quite still for a long moment, her arms
by her sides and her eyes closed. The sun lay warm and
caressing on her face, and drew from her tense limbs the
strain of the past days. She breathed deeply, taking in
the pungent fragrance of fallen leaves, the sweet odour
of ripe fruit in the small orchard beyond the lawn, the
subtle perfumes of the herbs behind the low box-hedge
to her right, all compounded with the scent of woodsmoke from a fire—a woodcutter's, perhaps—from the
closely growing woods outside the garden walls.

That was where she would go now, she decided,
knowing that it would be a little while at least before
they would think of looking for her there. A gate, almost
facing the door by which she had paused, led through

the high brick wall into the narrow lane which skirted it; and she let herself out to cross the track and hide herself quickly in the trees.

When she knew she was out of sight from the lane, Deborah slowed her pace to look about her. It was strange here, unfamiliar, a little frightening. Yet to a girl born and bred in London, alone in a wood for the first time in her life, it was a magical place, lit with flaming colours, haunted with dark shadows and secret corners, quiet and beautiful as a cathedral—though she knew that her puritan spirit should regard that as an unfavourable comparison.

In London she would have been afraid to wander in an unknown place without protection: city girl that she was, she knew well enough what dangers lurked even in the most busy streets—footpads, pickpockets, and worse. But of any dangers in the wood she knew nothing, for surely here she was likely to meet no one but a harmless woodman about his work, or an innocently passing traveller.

She wandered happily along mossy leaf-strewn paths, under beeches, past darkly gleaming hollies, disturbing small animals or birds as she went. Somewhere, distantly, she heard the woodcutters at their work, from the direction of the woodsmoke she had smelt from the garden. Deliberately, she took paths which led her away from them, delighting most of all in the new and entrancing sensation of being entirely alone.

Not that she had never been by herself, without others near, before: though even that was a rare enough experience. But not once in her life until now had she been allowed, by herself or by others, to pass her time without some definite task to do. From her earliest years she had learned that life was not made to be idled away in senseless pleasure. If no duty presented itself for immediate attention, then one must be sought, most strenuously. 'The Devil makes work for idle hands,' they had all said, her mother and her aunt, and all the ministers of religion and the preachers who had instructed her over the years. And she knew, a little guiltily, that she was indulging at the moment in exactly that senseless pleasure which had always been utterly condemned.

Her sense of guilt gave an added spice to her enjoyment of this forbidden fruit. It was as if that undoubtedly wicked decision she had made when she left the house had opened a door to a new kind of freedom. There was no one here to tell her what she must do. Each time she came on a new path she was faced with a moment of choice, and the awareness that she had only her own fancy to guide her. It was intoxicating, exhilarating.

After a while she began, softly and tentatively, to sing. It was the first time since she was a tiny child that she had sung anywhere but in church, and she knew nothing to sing now but psalms. But she sang the solemn words as lightly and trippingly as any young girl singing a country love song, because she was happy.

Once she paused to watch a robin hopping into the sunlight in an unexpected clearing. Once she saw a squirrel scampering out of sight into the copper foliage of a beech tree. And still she went on, along one enticing path after another, finding countless small things to delight her on the way.

She realised eventually that for some time now she had been making her way steadily uphill. At almost the same instant she realised with equal certainty that she was lost.

She stood turning and looking about her for any familiar feature. But she could not remember in any helpful detail how she had come to be here. The trees closed in on every side, threaded by little twisting paths all remarkably similar in appearance. She was not even quite sure exactly which one she had just come along to bring her here. She began for the first time to think of the punishment which must await her when she came home to her uncle's house. In the end, fighting the sudden panicky beating of her heart, she went on, towards the top of the hill. Just possibly there might be a clearing, a space large enough to give her a view. From there she might be able to discover which way she should go.

The trees did end just beyond the highest point of the rise, and there was a view. But for several moments she was so overcome with astonishment that all thoughts of her predicament left her completely.

Below her feet the land fell steeply away into a deep sheltered valley. The woods reached hazily purple-blue to its edge, and then grass, brilliantly green and velvet soft, spread to the valley floor, ornamented at intervals with carefully grouped plantations of trees. And there, in the very heart and centre of this secret valley, like a jewel in its case, stood a small castle. It rested, as if it were scarcely real, like something in a fairy tale, not on the harsh line of a defensive moat, but on a wide shining motionless expanse of water in which every line was mirrored with sharp clarity. To complete the perfection of the vision, a swan glided in smooth silence across the still surface of the water, the only moving thing in that flawless scene.

But it was flawed after all, Deborah saw in a moment. In her amazement and wonder she had seen the castle as a perfect whole, but that had been a short-lived illusion. She saw now that the towers and walls—strong, apparently invincible—ended abruptly and crudely after a few feet in sharp and jagged ruin.

Already plants were beginning to take root on the fallen stonework; but for all that it could not have been very long ago that the castle had been destroyed.

She shivered suddenly, with something of the sensation of someone finding a maggot at the heart of an apparently perfect fruit. And yet—it was beautiful even now, this hidden valley, and the lake crossed by the half-broken drawbridge. She was tempted against all commonsense to descend the slope and explore the damaged beauty below, half-expecting it to evaporate like a dream in the morning as she came nearer. But it must be almost dinner time, she thought, and she dared not put off the inevitable retribution any longer. As quickly as she could she must find her way home.

The decision was easily made, but that was as far as it went. The clearing so suddenly found had given her no clue at all as to which was the right path. She stood, hesitating, the anxiety rising in her again; and then saw the distant figure of a rider on horseback emerging, as if in response to her increasing panic, from the trees at the far side of the valley.

If his road did not lie this way he would disappear into the woods at some other point. She was too far away to run to meet him before he could go: she must somehow attract his attention. She cupped her hands about her mouth and shouted as loudly as she could, and then stood waving in the not-very-confident hope that he would see her. Then there was nothing to do but wait, with the uncomfortable thought coming to her that perhaps she had acted very foolishly in calling to him. After all, she could see only that the rider was a man—what kind of man she could not judge at this distance, and she was young, and female, and entirely alone.

For good or ill he had seen her, unless he had in any case been coming this way; for, gathering speed, he rode down and past the castle and the lake (they did not vanish as he passed, more unreal still though they looked with that prosaic intruder alongside), and then steadily approached her up the slope, along a track faintly marked on the short, dewy turf.

Deborah watched closely, trying to gauge what kind of man he was. Soberly dressed, certainly, in dark grey, with a severe black steeple-crowned hat on his head, but it was the sobriety of the Puritan, not the countryman. His heavy straight brown hair was cut off untidily just below the ears, with no concession to vanity; but his face, she saw as he came nearer, was grave but kindly, softened by quiet grey eyes. He was not old—about thirty perhaps—and not very tall, though well made, and she had a tantalising sense that she had seen him somewhere before. At least he looked safe enough, and she relaxed and moved to meet him as he came towards her.

He drew rein at her side and removed his hat, his eyes looking her over, uncritically and without emotion, simply trying to place her in some appropriate mental niche.

'Good day to you, mistress,' he said. 'Are you in need of assistance? I thought I saw you trying to attract my attention.'

'Yes,' said Deborah. 'I'm sorry to bring you out of your way. But I'm lost.'

'Then I shall be only too happy if I am able to help. Where do you wish to be?'

'At Pembridge Hall, my uncle's house,' she said, wondering if she could truthfully say it was where she wanted to be.

She saw the greater interest light his eyes.

'Indeed? Then there is no problem. I was on my way there myself. I am Robert Fanshawe, minister of this parish. And you? Master Foster's niece, did you say?'

'Deborah Halsey, sir.' That then was where she had
seen him, in church on Sunday. Clearly he found her
less memorable still, for even now he showed no recog-
nition. He nodded, though, for her name meant something to him.

'Ah, yes. I remember.'

The heiress, he was thinking. Recently orphaned and
come to live with her nearest surviving relatives. And
very soon to be wed to Sir Edward Biddulph, also some
sort of distant relation. 'Keeping the fortune in the
family,' he had thought uncharitably. He had seen her
in church, aware only of a bent head and clasped hands,
too insignificant to disturb the mental picture he had
formed of her when he first heard of her existence.

She was plain, they'd told him, in need of a firm
hand, but not a bad girl. The last two points he had no
means of judging as yet—though what was she doing
walking alone in the woods?—but of the first he was not
sure. Prim she certainly looked, in her grey gown and
white neckerchief, her pale face framed in that severe
white coif. She lacked colour too, and had the silent
repressed look he would have expected to find in Henry
Foster's niece; but the large dark long-lashed eyes
raised to his were very fine, and there was one stray curl
of hair, glossy and almost black, showing beneath the
wide fold of the cap. She was small and slight and
nervous, and yet he sensed that given love, and happiness, there might be something more there.

However, he must remember that he was not simply
a man, but a minister, and that the Fosters were among
his most devout and worthy parishioners. It was true
that there was something about them which made him
unable to regard them with anything more than a
rather distant respect, but he would have found it
difficult to say exactly in what, if anything, they fell
short as far as their Christian duty went.

'And what brought you out in the woods by yourself?' he asked. He saw the little flicker of apprehension in her eyes before she spoke. She knew, then, that she should not be here.

'It was so bright, and I wanted to be alone for a while——'

Robert Fanshawe resisted the temptation to put into words the sympathy he felt for her, imagining her day after day in that grimly pious household. These golden woods must have seemed like paradise to her, unused to them as she was.

'Weren't you afraid to wander here alone?' he asked, and in spite of himself there was more warmth than he intended in his voice.

'No,' she replied. 'Or at least, not until I knew I was lost.'

'Then you ought to have been,' he reprimanded her. 'It may all look very pretty, but it's a very good hiding place for all kinds of rogues who know their way about better than most honest folks. You're lucky to have come as far as this without mishap.'

For a moment she looked fearfully about her, and he smiled his reassurance.

'Never fear. You're safe enough now. But I wonder your aunt didn't warn you——Or didn't she know you came out?' he asked sharply, watching her expression.

'No,' Deborah admitted. 'I know it was very wrong of me.'

'There are worse sins,' he said cheerfully, to her surprise, and then went on in a brisk tone: 'But we'd best get you home as quickly as we can. Dan here's a good horse. He'll carry two.'

He dismounted and lifted her on to the saddle, rather precariously perched so that he could remount behind her.

'There now. We'll do for a short way.' He laughed

suddenly. 'I only hope none of my parishioners sees me like this!'

It was a diverting thought to Deborah that this man of God, of whom she had heard her aunt and uncle speak approvingly (though he was young, and a bachelor, two qualities which they felt he was duty bound to rectify as soon as possible), should be amused at the possibility of being caught in an improper situation. Ministers, in her previous experience, had always been men of unvarying dignity, who felt that nothing they did could be thought of as anything but seemly.

Master Fanshawe urged the big brown horse gently down the slope. His arm held her firmly, close enough for Deborah to be uncomfortably aware of his nearness. But there was no threat in his protective strength, and when she realised after a moment or two that they were passing the castle, the last traces of her embarrassment faded.

From close by she could see how sadly it had fallen into decay and how fine it must once have been. It filled her with a great sadness to see the gardens edging its walls overrun with weeds to the lake's rim, the rubble heaped on what had once been flower beds among the untended roses. 'What happened there?' she asked boldly, her curiosity overcoming her sense of decorum.

'A relic of the Civil Wars,' he said. 'It belonged to Lord Lenoyer, until he was killed at Naseby fight, then his heir Nicholas held it for the king. It was almost the last stronghold to fall. He was only sixteen, but a brave lad, and resourceful. They say it would never have been taken but for treachery within the walls. They didn't want to risk it being held again, so it was left as you see. It's said to be haunted.'

'Oh!' said Deborah, glancing again at the sunlit ruin as if she half-expected to see a headless ghost emerge. Behind her the minister laughed.

'They always say that about deserted buildings, especially castles and great houses. I imagine the ghost population has multiplied a hundredfold since the war, with so many Royalists overseas and their houses left to rack and ruin.'

'What happened to young Lord Lenoyer?'

'He escaped, I think, and went abroad. I imagine he's part of that unsavoury court in exile around Charles Stuart,' he added with distaste.

'And yet you admired what he did,' Deborah pointed out, for she had noticed the tone in which he had spoken of the incident.

'I admire courage and honour, however misguided,' he said. 'But the Royalist cause lost all that a long time ago, and that was all it ever had in its favour. What have it got now? Intrigue and debauchery, and little else. You can be sure that if ever—which God forbid—they bring Charles Stuart back, it'll be those qualities which will mark his rule. At least his father, for all his faults, was a man of strict morality. The son is quite another matter. But there, I cannot believe God allowed our cause to triumph only to bring it down to destruction—Here,' he went on, changing to a more practical tone, 'we've come to the road. Not far now.' He could feel the tension in her beneath his supporting arm, and tried to distract her from the thought of what she must face when she reached home. 'You are a Londoner, are you not?'

'Yes,' she said, 'I was born and bred there.'

'You will find it very different here in the country, I expect,' he said, 'not being used to country ways.'

'It doesn't seem very different,' she observed rather mournfully. 'Except today,' she added.

'It's a grand time of year, this,' he agreed. 'But then I think each season has its beauty. You will come to enjoy them all, I'm sure, more than you could in the city.'

'The air's sweeter anyway,' Deborah said, finding something to praise, and they both laughed. Feeling the amusement vibrating through her, Robert did all he could to keep her laughing until they came to Pembridge Hall. Within sight of its neat stone façade he knew that he could do no more to lighten her mood. She was home.

CHAPTER
TWO

DEBORAH had no illusion as to what her reception would be, and she was not disappointed. Her uncle took the minister discreetly on one side, while her aunt remained only long enough to thank him for returning their niece to them before bearing her upstairs to her own austere little parlour.

'What you need now, my girl,' she said as soon as she had closed the door, 'is a thorough whipping. What kind of spawn of the devil will the minister think you, now he has found you romping idle and aimless in the woods like any common gipsy? What would your dear mother say, if she were here to see you now?'

'She would have given me the whipping,' thought Deborah ruefully.

'Do you want us to be thought unfit to have the care of you? What if Sir Edward came to hear of it? What then?'

'What indeed?' thought Deborah wearily, her head bent.

She wondered if he were perhaps the kind of man who might, now and then, allow her some little harmless freedom—but then she supposed wandering in the woods was unlikely to be regarded as harmless by anyone. She did not know: her experience, she realised, had been very limited. Though surely, somewhere, there were people to whom not every pleasure was forbidden? Even the minister had laughed. . . .

'As it happens I shall not whip you,' her aunt went on. 'But not, be it said, because I am weak. I am not one to shirk my clear duty. However, I do not wish you to meet Sir Edward for the first time, sore from a whipping. Instead you will remain in your room without food until morning. And never again, while you are under this roof, will you spend one moment unattended or unsupervised. If you cannot be trusted to have the necessary strength of character to do what is right, then the deficiency must be supplied by others.'

To her room then Deborah went, and sat alone at the window listening to her aunt turning the key in the lock and walking away along the passage to make herself pleasant to the minister.

Not that the punishment was so terrible as her aunt clearly anticipated. The thought of the long days ahead of her, when she must never be left by herself, not for one moment, was a grim one. But that time would not be unending, for in a month she would be married; and surely as a wife and mistress of a household she would no longer be treated as a heedless girl. As for today, it was almost pleasant to sit here by herself and remember the excitements of the morning, fast fading in her mind to the unreality of a dream. After all, it was so very unlike her to have behaved so recklessly——

By breakfast time the next morning Deborah was thoroughly hungry, and resigned once more to the meek demeanour from which she had so unexpectedly strayed yesterday. At household prayers before breakfast, her uncle had appealed loudly to the Lord to break the stubborn spirit of His child Deborah, having reminded Him as a preliminary exactly what her fault had been. 'Just to be sure,' thought Deborah, 'that everyone from the kitchen boy upwards knows what I have done.'

But that was over now, and there was bread and small beer to stay her hunger, and then her aunt stood

by critically while Nan dressed her to meet her betrothed. Her best black gown this time, heavy silk with
a discreet touch of lace at cuffs and collar, and edging
the coif into which every strand of hair was so ruthlessly
pushed that Deborah's head began to ache.

For all her fine clothes she did not look at her best
today, Nan thought, for she was white and strained and
anxious, standing meekly under the lashing tongue of
her aunt, who was concerned that if her niece disgraced
her it should not be by any negligence on her part. Nan
hoped fervently that Sir Edward was a kindly man who
would love her mistress: she suspected that she alone, a
mere servant, was the only person who had ever loved
Deborah.

They were to travel in style today in the family coach,
an old and draughty vehicle which Deborah felt was the
least comfortable mode of transport ever devised. Her
uncle was to ride alongside, together with four of the
household's male servants. Deborah was surprised at
such an excessive escort for a six-mile journey, but had
long ago learned not to question her elders, even on
what was simply a matter of interest. Fortunately for
her curiosity, her aunt supplied the answer unasked.

'We can't be too careful these days,' she said, as she
placed herself at her niece's side in the coach. 'There
was no trouble on these roads while the Lord Protector
was alive, but these days——'

'Highwaymen, madam?' put in Nan, bolder than her
mistress.

'That's too courteous a word,' declared Susan
Foster. 'As the minister says, there's many an old
soldier from the King's armies calling himself "Captain
this" or "Captain that", just so he'll be thought more
than a common thief, who sets on respectable citizens
even in broad daylight. And none of them more than
the riffraff of the army, not an officer among them.

Captain Black, the one in these parts calls himself—the biggest rogue unhung, too. In Oliver's day he'd not have lasted five minutes—but then those days are gone, alas.'

Deborah, who felt she had enough to trouble her in her day-to-day life without worrying about highwaymen, gave her attention to watching the scenery from the window, and allowed her aunt's regrets for days gone by to flow over her unheard.

The road led for the most part over heathland, thickly covered with bracken and gorse, and through woods; but it was a bright morning, and there was nothing in the brilliance of the autumn day to cause anxiety to the travellers, beyond the extreme roughness of the roads.

By the time they reached Sandwell, Deborah, who had eaten very little over the past forty-eight hours, was feeling faint and exhausted. But she had sufficient pride not to allow her weariness to show, except in the unavoidable pallor of her complexion and the bruised smudges beneath her eyes. She dismounted from the coach with head held high, and then paused, to take in the grandeur of the Elizabethan mansion which was to be her future home. It was beautiful, the brick rosy in the sunlight, the gardens fragrant and alive with colour, and she felt a sudden surge of optimism.

Then, down the shallow flight of steps from the porch of the house, came a man, slowly and with dignity. He was tall and broad-shouldered with light reddish hair, already greying, and a complexion oddly close in colour to the bricks of his house. He was dressed inevitably, as Deborah had expected, in the sober unadorned dark green of a man who had rejected wordly vanity. That told her only that in religion and politics he was probably in sympathy with her uncle. In her more fanciful moments she had dreamed of finding her betrothed to be handsome, or at least attractive. That, it seemed at first glance, he was not. But if he was kind and considerate it would be enough. She was not so foolish as to hope for love.

Sir Edward came nearer and greeted her aunt and uncle, and then turned to her a little awkwardly, and yet with the same stateliness with which he seemed to accomplish any task. They stood for a moment looking at each other. Deborah saw that his eyes were small, rather close together, light and fair-lashed. She did not much care for them, but she knew better than to judge by appearances. She bent her head, and curtsied, and then he bowed and drew her arm through his.

'Let us go inside,' he said. 'Dinner is ready; but first you must make the acquaintance of my mother.'

His mother: that she had not expected. She imagined, hopefully, a frail old lady, long past housewifely cares, happy to bask in the loving attentions of her daughter-in-law and to love her in return.

In the parlour to which they were led stood a lady as tall as her son, upright, stern-jawed, formidably severe in her dress and her expression, who studied Deborah in silence from head to foot and back again for several seconds before she spoke. When at last she did speak, it was to Deborah's aunt she turned.

'Will she make my son a good wife, do you think, cousin?'

'I think so,' said Mistress Foster, though Deborah suspected she was concealing her true feelings. 'She is young and still, of course, much in need of training. But from you and Sir Edward she will, I know, have all the guidance and instruction she needs.'

Deborah felt those pale sharp eyes travel over her once more.

'A little undersized, perhaps. A little too narrow in the hips to be sure of safe child-bearing. But we can hope for the best. Is she healthy? Does she ail much?'

'Very little, so I gather,' Susan reassured her.

'They will look at my teeth next,' thought Deborah, with a little tremor of amusement stirring within the depths of her new, and complete, despair. Here, she knew, was no hope for the future; no remote possibility of sympathy or love. From a stern unbending father and a rigid and uncaring mother she had come to an equally unloving uncle and aunt; she was now to pass into the hands of this woman, who seemed to hold distilled within her the essence of all those harsh adults who had reared her, and to become the wife of this man who was her son and only too clearly cast in her mould.

'She will, I am sure,' her aunt was saying, 'endeavour always to do her duty.'

'That's what they'll write on my tomb,' thought Deborah: '*She did her duty*. It's all they'll be able to write, because that is my life. There will never be anything more.'

The food at dinner was as plain and sober as could be expected, and the conversation ponderous and slow under Sir Edward's direction. It was clear, thought Deborah, that his mother ruled the household, but that he ruled her. There at least there was love, the doting, blind, utterly exclusive love of the mother for an only son, which the son clearly took entirely for granted. No woman, Deborah knew, would ever be good enough for Sir Edward in his mother's eyes: least of all a quiet, meek, unformed seventeen-year-old, who wanted only to be loved.

After dinner they were subjected to a conducted tour of the house. Everything seemed to be designed to impress Deborah with the formidable efficiency of its mistress—no speck of dust would have dared to settle on the shining oak treads of the stairs below Dame Arbella Biddulph's feet, no spider to construct its web in the corners of the spotless panelling.

There was one surprise only, in a small insignificant room at the far end of the west wing. It was clearly never used, though as thoroughly clean as every other part of the house, but in a dark corner hung a portrait, unmistakably a likeness of Sir Edward in his younger days.

It was so surprising a portrait that Deborah paused before it, studying the curling lovelocks portrayed there, the rich velvet and lace of the doublet, the sword supported by the jauntily tied scarlet sash, the battle scene in the background—with surely, in miniature on a distant hill, a tiny portrait of the late King Charles on a white charger.

The rest of the party had moved on, leaving her behind; and her aunt, noticing her absence, came to find her. For once, briefly, she was almost human.

'Sir Edward,' she whispered, in the tone of one disclosing a scandal, 'served the King once, early in the war. He fought at Edgehill—but of course,' she went on more briskly, 'he saw the error of his ways before it was too late, and retired to his estates. Since then he has been a loyal servant of God and Parliament.'

It occurred to Deborah to wonder why the revealing portrait had not been destroyed—and then, cynically, illumination dawned. Of course, if at any time the King were to return, it would supply excellent proof of Sir Edward's loyalty. That he was dull, elderly and unsympathetic she had already begun to learn. It looked as though he was also a man whose guiding principle was his own self-interest. It was not a cheering thought.

Unfortunately, Aunt Susan's moment of weakness in repeating her crumb of gossip cost her more than a slight lowering of dignity in the eyes of her niece. The two of them hurried after the rest of the party, by now already descending the stairs, and at the head of those glowing polished steps Aunt Susan slipped, lost her balance, and fell, clumsily twisting her way past the others to land on the flagged floor at the foot, an untidy crumpled heap on the hard and spotless surface.

Deborah was the first to gather her wits and run to her aunt. All her considerable thwarted powers of compassion and love were centred on that figure lying there. She knelt at her side, taking her aunt's hand and calling her name agitatedly. She was full of concern, unheeding the others gathered about her, though they were calling sharp orders to servants and to herself. Her relief when almost at once her aunt stirred and groaned and opened her eyes was immeasurable.

'Lie still, dear aunt,' she urged, as Susan Foster tried to raise herself. 'You must lie still. Madam'—she turned to Dame Arbella—'have you a blanket I could lay over her? I am sure she should not be moved yet.'

Her dark eyes were alive with compassion and concern. Sir Edward, watching her, felt the first stirrings of attraction. He was by nature too self-centred to love; but that appealing gaze, the clear-complexioned countenance flushed with emotion, the firm young breasts rising and falling rapidly with Deborah's anxious breathing, aroused a new interest in him. His mother had seen it too, and, watching him, was at once on her guard.

'Edward, my son, there is a cloak in the parlour.'

He needed no further prompting, though he cast a final glance at Deborah before he hurried to follow his mother's hint. 'Of course. I will bring it at once.'

Deborah, it seemed, had not even been aware of his interest. Her attention was concentrated on her aunt, who was completely conscious now, and full of breathless apologies for the inconvenience she was causing. She resisted her niece's attempts to prevent her from moving, and by the time Sir Edward returned with the cloak was halfway to her feet.

It was not a wise move, for it caused her to place her considerable weight on an injured ankle, and at the next moment crumple with a moan into unconsciousness.

They carried her to the parlour and laid her on the long cushioned windowseat, and covered her with the cloak. Deborah, aware that there was little of a positive nature she could do, devoted herself to sitting on a stool at her aunt's side, stroking her hair. That, she was sure, was the kind of unobtrusive solace she would have appreciated in Susan Foster's situation.

The surgeon was sent for and by the time he had arrived and examined Mistress Foster, and declared that she had suffered no worse injury than a sprained ankle and some measure of shock, it was late in the afternoon. By now they should have set out on their return journey, but the surgeon, having bound the ankle, advised that Susan should have a night's rest before attempting to go home.

Dame Arbella took control, ordering the best spare bedroom to be made ready for her guests; and then turning to ask Henry Foster if he would remain with his wife, or accompany his niece back to Pembridge.

'But I must stay,' Deborah broke in, abandoning her meek unobtrusiveness. 'My aunt has need of me.'

She longed, with a desperation far greater than the situation merited, for her aunt to agree that she was indispensable to her comfort; but Mistress Foster only said wearily, 'Dame Arbella will care for me quite well, I'm sure. But Henry must stay: I must have him near me in case I should be taken worse. If you've no room for Deborah, then Tom and William can ride back with her. She'll be safe in their hands with the maid for company. They can bring the coach back for me tomorrow.'

'It is not that we have insufficient space,' put in
Dame Arbella, rejecting the adverse reflection on her
house. 'But I do not think it fitting,' she went on in a low
voice, just audible to Deborah but not to her son, who
had accompanied the surgeon to the door, 'for her to
remain in the house with Sir Edward until they are
safely wed. She is young, and you know how it is with
young girls, if they are exposed too readily to temptation.'

It took Deborah a moment or two to realise, with
amazement, that Dame Arbella fully expected her, in
the intoxicating circumstance of spending a night
under the same roof with her betrothed, to do all in her
power to seduce him. She, of course, had not seen the
earlier gleam of interest in Sir Edward's eye; but even if
she had, the thought that she should for a moment be
tempted to make advances to him was a ludicrous one.
But she could see that to Dame Arbella it was a very
real possibility.

There was no whisper of protest from her aunt, no
concern on her behalf from her uncle, at the prospect of
Deborah's travelling over six miles of lonely road at
dusk with half the escort which had seemed essential to
a larger party in broad daylight. Not that she was
afraid, simply hurt that she should mean so little to
them. Yet it was, after all, a painfully familiar situation
to her, this putting of morals and discipline and cor-
rectness of behaviour before any of the demands of
affection or love. She had long ago realised that love
was not for her, however much she might long for it at
heart.

She took her leave of them with the restrained good
manners she had been trained to show, and she and
Nan climbed into the coach as it began slowly to move
away from the house, the two servants on horseback at
either side.

It would not be fully dark for an hour yet, but the sun was low and the shadows heavy under the trees. The coach passed first along a road through the woodlands which sheltered the Sandwell fields. Then the land rose steeply, and the horses struggled up the hill to the open space of heathland at its summit. Here it was lighter, but the woods which fringed the heath were dark and impenetrable. The coach went slowly, because the horses were tired now, and there was less urgent need for speed where the land edging the road was open, covered with bracken and scrub but nothing which could conceal a man on a horse.

It was then that it happened. The first warning of trouble to reach Deborah and Nan was the sound of a shot, fired at some distance; and then the confused noise of thudding hooves and a horse neighing in terror.

The next thing they knew was that the coach was moving along at an incredible, dangerous speed, rocking drunkenly over the ruts and holes in the road, swaying and jolting as if the devil himself were driving.

Deborah caught Nan's eye, and saw her own anxiety reflected there. It was an accident they feared, for clearly the coachman or the servants had made a rather foolhardy attempt to throw off their unwelcome pursuer, rather than to remain and confront him. Perhaps it had been 'them', rather than 'him', and any other course had seemed hopeless, with so few of them to protect the coach.

'I think I'd sooner be robbed than break my neck,' Deborah said, with one of her ironic flashes of humour.

She dragged herself to the window and leaned out, holding desperately to the swaying sides of the coach. A glance was all she could manage without falling, and it did not help. She could see no one, not even the outriding servants, though she thought she heard

hoofbeats following behind the coach; and she dared
not lean further out to call to the coachman. In any
case, with the hooves thundering and wheels rattling as
they did, he would very likely not have heard her.

She sank back on to the seat, hurled against Nan as
she did so. 'We must be clear of them now. Why doesn't
he stop?' she gasped.

'Perhaps he can't,' suggested Nan.

Perhaps not; perhaps the horses had taken fright at
the shot and the coachman could no longer control
them. The two women closed their eyes, clutched the
seat, and sat dizzyingly praying for the nauseating
movement to cease.

They were passing through the woods again now,
and it was almost completely dark. The coach suddenly
gave a greater jolt and swayed, and then lurched
dangerously almost on to its side. Then, the corner
passed too quickly for safety, it righted itself in the nick
of time, and slowed very slightly. It was still moving
much faster than comfort and prudence should have
allowed, but after the breakneck speed of its pace before
it was something of a relief. Though not to Nan.

'If we go on like this I shall be sick,' she vowed.

Mercifully, after a few moments more, the coach
rocked and swerved, and halted, abruptly, throwing its
occupants to the floor.

'Thank God,' was all Nan had breath to say, as
Deborah reached to open the door and release her
white-faced maid into the air.

She had laid her hand on the door when it was
opened from outside. She was about to express her
thanks for that courtesy and for the uncomfortable
rescue, when the words died in her throat.

There before her was not the quiet twilit façade of
Pembridge, and William bowing to her to step down;
but simply the trees, dusky and unending. Against

them stood two darker figures, one short, one tall; featureless behind masks, hats low over their eyes, the shorter of them holding a lantern so that the two in the coach could see clearly the pistol held in the hand of the taller. A pistol levelled menacingly, straight at Deborah.

Nan, sickness forgotten, screamed. The pistol moved a fraction. 'One more sound from you,' said a quiet, incisive voice, 'and I fire.'

The door opened wider, and the tall man bowed exaggeratedly.

'Step down, both of you—Sim, the lantern.'

The light was moved closer and the two women inspected, slowly. The tall man spoke to Nan at last.

'You're the servant? Right, back into the coach. You will be returned to Pembridge. There you will tell Master Henry Foster that you bring word to him from Captain Black. You will tell him that unless he comes, alone and unarmed, with two thousand pounds, to the crossroads by the crooked oak at midnight tomorrow, he will find his niece in Sandwell mere with a sack of rocks about her neck. You understand?'

Silenced by fear and horror, Nan nodded. Deborah, numbed and motionless, watched as if it were nothing at all to do with her. The coach door slammed shut, the lantern was extinguished, the shorter man mounted to the box, and the coach was driven away. She looked on as if she were seeing it all by chance from a window.

And then the horrible reality of it caught shudderingly at her. Nan had gone, and she was alone in the darkness with an armed man at her side.

CHAPTER
THREE

IT took Deborah a few seconds to come out of that dreadful moment of awareness, and to be urged to action. As the last sound of the departing coach faded into the darkness, she turned sharply and began to run with the unthinking speed of panic back along the dim road away from her captor. It was a useless action, a heedless one which would have been without point even if she had known where she could go. For, of course, the tall man had been mounted. It was his horse whose hooves she had heard behind the coach, and now he was in the saddle and after her almost at once. Even on foot he would without doubt have caught her, for she stumbled on the heavy silk of her skirts, tearing the hem, and almost fell as he reached her. She screamed, instinctively and helplessly, and then was swept up into the saddle before him and held ruthlessly in place.

For a moment she had a brief painful recollection of that ride only yesterday: twice in two days, on horseback with a man. But yesterday's escapade had been fun, a little uncomfortable perhaps, but agreeable, something to remember with pleasure. This was unmitigated horror: no tentative supporting arm here, no consideration for her modesty or his reputation, simply a harsh unyielding clasp from which Deborah knew there was no escape. Even to cry out was pointless, and he reminded her of it at once, that crisp voice close to her ear:

'Scream all you like, sweeting. There's no one to hear.'

She could not have screamed now if she had wished

to, with that chill trickle of fear running down her spine
at his tone. She tried not to think of it, of the dreadful
loneliness of her situation; but it was worse a little later
when the words he had spoken to Nan began to repeat
themselves in her head: 'He will find his niece in Sandwell mere with a sack of rocks about her neck.' She had
no doubt that he meant it.

She did not know how long they travelled like this,
and it was some time before she was aware of anything
at all but her fear. Then she began to wonder if her
captor had any idea where he was going, threading his
way in the dark through the trees, often bending
beneath a branch, crushing her harshly as he did so.
Perhaps he would lose his way, and they would emerge
from the trees somewhere where she was known, where
she could call for help. But she did not really hope that
this might happen, because she knew it was impossible.
No man would have taken the risk he had in abducting
her, to endanger it all by losing his way in the woods.
She had no real doubt at all that he knew exactly where
he was going.

The path twisted and turned, rose and fell, and still
the trees seemed endless, growing darker and less hos-
pitable. There would be no delight in wandering among
them now, even free and out of danger.

Then he drew rein with a quiet word to his horse, in a
gentle tone quite unlike that he had used to her, she
noticed. Her heart beat faster, wondering what would
happen now: she could see no sign of a house or any
shelter but the trees, though perhaps that was because
it was too dark to see.

He made no move to dismount, and his arm if anything tightened about her; but she did not have long to
wonder why he had halted. She felt his other arm move
behind her and then rise again, and in a moment he was
tying something roughly across her eyes. A blindfold, so

that she should not be able to describe his hideout, if ever she were free to tell.

It was thick, impenetrable, but of some fine soft fabric so that it did not hurt her, for all the manner in which it was tied. Deborah was beginning to reflect that with hands free she could pull it from her face in spite of him, when clearly that seemed to occur to him also. Her arms were drawn back and something else, rope this time, was tied about her wrists. She made one brief and useless attempt to struggle, but it only caused the horse to sidle nervously, and she was too afraid of falling to risk anything more. It was a very large horse, and the ground a long way off, down there in the total blackness.

So, bound and blindfolded, she felt the arm go about her again and the horse move forward. She listened now, intent for any sound which might indicate where she was. They went briefly uphill, and then downhill for some time, and she thought from the lighter, freer sound of the hooves that the ground must be more open. Then the path levelled again and the hooves for a moment sounded loud on a hard surface—wood perhaps—and went a little further, and finally halted.

There was no escape now, she knew. She felt the small hardness of the pistol-barrel against her ribs as he dismounted, and that hated voice said softly: 'One wrong move and you're dead.'

That strange detached part of herself, which even now seemed untouched by the horror of her circumstances, thought ironically: 'You'd not get your money that way.' But there was no thought of disobedience in her, as he lifted her from the saddle and led her, pistol still at her ribs, along a rough stony path to an area which she sensed to be partially enclosed—by walls perhaps. Then she heard a key turn in a lock, a door creak slowly open, and she was urged forward.

'Take care on the steps,' he said, with neutral concern.

She moved slowly on, caught for a moment by some trailing plant, and then, guided by his hand, felt her way down the long steep flight of narrow steps on to which the door had opened. At the foot of the steps he said 'wait there', and she heard him run lightly up to secure the door behind them.

Then, and only then, he unbound her wrists and took the blindfold from her eyes. There was no need of it now, for they stood in total darkness.

Deborah reached out blindly for some familiar or recognisable object which might give her some clue as to what kind of place this was. On one side her hand found the cold damp shiny surface of a wall, so much like the traditional dungeon wall that she shuddered. Then, mercifully, there was a harsh rasping noise and a flame leapt up in the blackness, settling after a moment of hesitation into the steady light of a candle. It showed her dimly the tall figure of her captor, masked still and wearing a long disguising cloak, bent over the flame at a rough table, such as might be found in any poor cottage.

She looked round, noting the green glistening stonework of the walls: a small room, apparently windowless, with steps rising to the door. An earth floor, partially covered with well-trodden straw. Two stools at the table, and against a wall a low truckle bed, such as servants and children used, the only bedding a straw mattress and a rough blanket. It was an utterly cheerless sight.

The man turned then to look at her, and removed his hat with a gesture whose grace struck her even in that place. It was as if an inbred courtesy overcame any fear in him of being recognised or described, if she should ever be free to tell.

For she would not forget that hair, she knew that. It fell to his shoulders in a shining fairness such as she had rarely seen on any man, or any woman come to that: silken, curling a little at the point where it reached the darkness of the cloak, a brightness rivalling the candle. It made her gaze at him more carefully, observing the straight brows, oddly dark against that pale hair, which were visible above the makeshift mask, and the fair skin, naturally fair she thought, though a highwayman would not see much sunlight to darken his complexion.

It was a moment or two, in her surprise, before she remembered where she was and why. Then his voice broke in on her returning fear.

'Are you hungry?' he asked. 'I shall eat, and so will Sim when he comes back. But there's enough for three.'

'I'm not hungry,' she said, miserably feeling that she would never wish to eat again. And at the same time noting with that same surprise what she had not appreciated before: that his voice was without accent, quiet and cultured, and when not reminding her of her fate, pleasing to the ear. His hands, too, she saw as he reached across to set bread and cheese on the table, were slender and long-fingered: attractive hands.

Hands which would not hesitate to fill a sack to the brim with rocks, to make sure she would sink in the green waters of Sandwell mere beyond hope of rescue. Her own hands flew to her throat, and fear leapt up in her again, shutting out all interest in her captor.

'Perhaps you'd like to rest,' he suggested. 'Make yourself at home on the bed.'

Deborah looked round the room, and long years of dutiful self-abasement reasserted themselves.

'But there's only one bed,' she said. 'Where will you sleep?'

She was astonished when he laughed, softly and with genuine amusement.

'Oh my child, you have indeed been ill-used,' he said, 'if you feel you can't even accept that from me. But never fear: my motives are not so generous as you seem to think—we must keep you in health if we're to hope for a ransom for you. So the bed is yours. Make the most of it.'

She sat down rather suddenly on the hard prickly surface of the bed, and stared at him with a cruel lump in her throat. She was overwhelmed all at once by everything which had happened to her. Until now life had offered very little. No happiness, no joy, few small pleasures to remember; yet at this moment she would have given anything to return to that sombre tediousness again. Anything, rather than this fear, this horrible place, alone with a man who would murder her without mercy, without hesitation, only for money—for that one thing she had, the one thing she would blithely have given in return for all those other priceless commodities she had never known. Slowly, a tear rolled down her cheek, and then another, and another, glistening unmistakably in the dim light of the candle.

The man looked up, gave a sudden exclamation, and moved swiftly to her side.

'Come now, child;' he said, in a tone which mingled impatience and a faintly discernible concern. 'There's nothing to drive you to tears. You've a bed, and food, and you need have no more to do with me now you're here, until it's time to leave. Your uncle will find the money soon enough, and then you'll be free. Just a few hours from now, that's all. Here——' He held out a handkerchief to her, rather in the manner of an aloof bachelor faced with an infant whose ways he could not hope to understand. She took it miserably and blew her nose. 'Now get some sleep. It helps to pass the time.'

She obeyed him mechanically, and he dragged the blanket from beneath her and threw it casually over her.

Her physical needs concerned him, because he must have her alive and well for the moment when payment was made. But then, she was not used to any greater tenderness in those about her, so that the reflection did not chill her as it might have done. She lay with closed eyes, motionless but exhausted, yet aware that for some time he stood watching her before moving away to complete the arrangements for his meagre supper.

She did not sleep: she would have been surprised if she had, for all her weariness. She lay for some time as she had been when he left her, eyes closed, without moving. Then she opened them again and watched the man, wondering once more in a sleepy way how it was that he was so unlike the common idea of a highwayman, the uncouth brute of her imagination. Whatever he had done, or planned to do, he was clearly not that.

Then a hammering on the door jerked her fully awake. For a foolish moment she thought they had found her, and in a short while she would be safe. Then she realised, dismally, that it must be Sim, back from delivering Nan and her message at Pembridge. She watched as the door was opened—only very briefly, just long enough for Sim to slip inside—and the stocky figure of the other man, much more the conventional idea of a highwayman, came down the steps with her captor.

'They're not there, Captain. Not just now,' Sim was saying as he moved into the light: he too was still masked.

So, thought Deborah, noting the respectful manner in which Sim spoke to the other man, perhaps he really had been a Captain in the Royalist army, perhaps that explained the cultivated manner and speech which had so struck her.

'Seems Mistress Foster met with an accident at Sandwell and stayed there, and Master Foster with her.

They'll be home tomorrow—no, today it will be, won't it? This morning, so the servant woman said.'

'So that's why they gave us so little trouble,' observed the Captain. 'All to the good, in the circumstances. Presumably the woman will give them the message when they return.'

'So she said,' agreed Sim, 'and I think she meant it. She took on terrible-like at what had become of this one.'

Both men glanced across at Deborah, who returned their gaze mournfully.

'They'll pay up, never fear,' the Captain said with confidence, and added to Deborah, 'Go to sleep, child. You've nothing to fear.'

It seemed a pointless exhortation, when there was no hope that she would be able to rest in this place. And yet, once the two men were seated at the table, facing each other across it, eating and talking in low voices so that she could not hear the words, she found that her eyelids began gradually to feel heavy, leaden, and at last they closed against the light and she drifted into sleep before she knew that she would.

She awoke to a sleepy instant of doubt before the stark recollection of what had happened hit her with all its force. She wished then that she had not woken, but there was no likelihood that she might sleep again now. She turned her head to look about her, and realised that there must, after all, be a window in her prison: a small one, concealed in a corner and reached by a narrow shaft in the low vaulted ceiling, but enough to admit sufficient daylight now to show her the two sleeping figures on the damp straw covering the floor.

Sim lay on his back, his greying beard jutting aggressively into the air, moving with the rhythm of his snores. The Captain, rolled in his cloak, lay on his side, his unmasked face resting on one opened palm. Deborah felt an odd and unaccustomed sensation in the pit of her stomach as her eyes moved to that face, defenceless in sleep, the dark lashes curved on the fine cheekbones, the wide mouth relaxed beneath the long straight nose. He was older than she was, clearly: about thirty perhaps, but young enough to retain that look of innocence in repose, the fair skin unlined and flushed with faint colour.

She was watching him still, quite unable to do otherwise, when he stirred and opened his eyes, and her unruly stomach gave a great lurch as they met hers, dark, alert, observant as they were—the more striking against the fairness of his hair.

He watched her steadily for a moment, and she felt the colour rise to her hairline. Then he moved with lithe grace to his feet, and she remembered yesterday, sharply, and recoiled. He saw the flinching, and paused at the table's edge.

'Did you sleep well?' he asked, with the calm courtesy of a host addressing his guest after the first night passed under his roof.

'Yes,' she answered, almost inaudibly.

'Good. Now perhaps you can eat a little.'

She realised then, with some surprise, that she was hungry. She sat up, pushing the blanket aside, and swung her legs to the floor. In spite of the blanket, and the cloak she still wore over her gown, she was not very warm: she felt chilled and stale and uncomfortable after a night passed fully dressed in this damp place. She wondered briefly whether the Captain had been very cold with only his cloak for cover.

Breakfast seemed to consist of what remained from last night's meal: stale cheese, hard bread, sour ale. She was hungry enough when he brought it to her to find it at least a little satisfying, though she did not eat a great

deal. Always mindful of her manners, she thanked him
for it, and received a slight answering smile from the
man seated at the table. It gave a momentary softness
to his expression, and for that space of time she found it
hard to believe that this man would kill her without
compunction if her uncle did not hand over the money.
But there was no lasting reassurance, for the softness
went as quickly as it had come, and she remembered
the threat he had made, last night, and the gun held to
her ribs.

After an interval she realised that he was watching
her again, with his dark brows drawn together in a
slight frown. At last he asked casually, 'How was it you
did not stay at Sandwell with your aunt yesterday?'

'Because,' she said candidly, 'Dame Arbella was
afraid I might be an evil influence on Sir Edward.'

He looked puzzled.

'Oh? But I understood you were to marry him.'

'So I am,' she said, and it was strange that even now,
when she was in mortal danger, the thought still managed to depress her a little. 'But Dame Arbella evi-
dently did not trust me to be able to contain myself until
our wedding. Or perhaps she knows her son better than
I, and did not trust him.'

'From what I know of Sir Edward that is scarcely
likely. There is——' he stopped short and looked at
her, as if considering whether it was wise to go on.

'What do you know of him?' she asked sharply.

'Only what I have heard. In my position one relies on
gossip: an invaluable source of information. Sim is very
good at keeping his ear cocked in the alehouse. That is
how I knew you were an heiress, come to live with your
uncle; and how I knew you were to marry Sir Edward.
And how, too, I heard that you were to travel to Sandwell yesterday.'

She was silent for a moment, gazing down at her

clasped hands, considering. Then she looked up at him.

'And will you consider your two thousand pounds well earned when my uncle brings it to you?'

She saw in the dim light that he coloured slightly. Was he not, after all, entirely without scruples? She had no means of telling, for he left the question unanswered, gazing moodily past her into the shadowy corners of the room. Deborah wondered what he was thinking. There did not seem to be any point in pursuing the brief argument; though she would dearly have liked to know how a gentleman, as he clearly was, came to be earning his living in this way. But then so many Royalists had lost everything in the King's cause that perhaps it was not so surprising after all. That was something it might be more tactful for her not to probe, Puritan as she was, though too young to have played any part in the war.

Instead she began to wonder about the alehouse gossip which had proved so useful to him.

'What did they say about Sir Edward? And about me?' she asked.

He returned to his stool at the table.

'That you are a devout little Puritan, reared in a good Puritan household in London; that your father died a wealthy man and left all to you and to your mother, who is now also dead. That your uncle became your guardian, and arranged a very suitable match for you with Sir Edward Biddulph, who is some kind of kin of yours—All of which is, I imagine, no mere gossip, but quite true.'

'What then of the gossip?' asked Deborah. 'What do they say of Sir Edward? What kind of man is he thought to be?'

'That,' said the Captain guardedly, 'I think I must leave to you to discover for yourself. You are, after all, to be his wife.'

'Then what you have heard is not to his credit?'

'I only know that he is—shall we say—a prudent man. Careful where his own advantage is concerned. He would not die for a principle, of that I am sure. But in a husband I expect that is an asset.'

'Perhaps,' agreed Deborah, without conviction. She remembered that portrait, half concealed, but ready in case it should one day prove useful. That, to a man whose loyalty (she supposed) to a lost cause had reduced him to robbery on the highway, must make Sir Edward Biddulph wholly unappealing.

Some part of her, in spite of her situation, found itself in sympathy with the Captain's distaste. She wondered if her captor knew of Sir Edward's past indiscretion in support of the King; but some sense of loyalty to a man who had shown her no kindliness at all prevented her from speaking of it.

They had both fallen silent when Sim awoke and scrambled to his feet. The Captain looked round and motioned him to the table. 'Come to breakfast, Sim.'

'I'll see to the horses first, Captain,' said Sim. The Captain let him out at the door at the top of the steps, and re-locked it. This must be a very secluded place, Deborah thought, if horses could be safely concealed here.

When Sim returned, and the two men sat down to their breakfast, she realised that the Captain had not eaten with her, but waited until the servant had fed the horses, to share his meal. She remembered Nan's remark about those who used those about them as if they were as much God's children as themselves. It was surprising to her that the Captain should be in that category—would Nan have approved of him? she wondered with a little ironical smile.

The day passed slowly. The men played cards, in which Deborah declined to join them, and slept a little, generally taking turns to do so—though scrupulously

leaving the bed for her use. They seemed to have come
to the end of the food, so there was no more to eat. In
what Deborah supposed from the state of the light to be
the early evening, Sim went out—to listen to his alehouse gossip, perhaps, for news of more rich Puritans to
plunder. He returned with a roast capon, a fresh-baked
loaf, and a flagon of good ale.

'A feast indeed,' said the Captain approvingly.
'Come, Mistress Halsey, and join us. It will be your last
dinner in our company.'

Because I will be free—or dead? she asked herself,
with a momentary lurch of fear. But she came to the
table all the same.

The Captain was in high spirits, presumably antici-
pating the fortune to be received at the crossroads at
midnight. Sim told them how the talk had all been of
the abducted heiress, and lurid in imaginative detail at
that—Deborah sensed that in consideration for her he
left out a great deal of what he had heard. The two
families most nearly concerned were said to be distraught, and had shut their doors to all comers but the
minister and a Captain of dragoons who had now set
out with a detachment of men to scour the countryside
for the notorious Captain Black.

The Captain laughed at that, and raised his tankard.

'Then here's to them all! May they live and prosper.
But to us most of all—in which,' he added, with a
smiling glance at Deborah, 'I include you, of course, the
ultimate source of our impending prosperity.'

After the meal the two men prepared to go out, and
Deborah realised with horror that she was to be left
here alone. Any company, she felt, was better than that.

But they did at least leave her a candle, and the
Captain reassured her as they moved to the door.

'We'll not be long, child. Don't be troubled.'

It was small comfort, once the key had turned behind

them and she was left to the dripping silence of her prison. She could not even hear the departing hooves from here.

What, she thought, in sudden terrible panic, if the men were confronted by the dragoons and killed? What then would become of her, locked away with no one to tell where she was? Would they find her in a hundred years, a mouldering skeleton, dead of fear and starvation?

She tried to control herself, to order her thoughts into less terrifying channels, but the little mental picture of herself in the total darkness left by the spent candle, hammering despairingly, endlessly, on the door, unheard and unheeded, would not leave her.

She stood up and wandered about to examine her prison from corner to corner. Perhaps there would be some way out. She found the shaft where the window was set, but the space was tiny and rigidly barred. If Sim and the Captain died, or escaped without talking, she would be here for the rest of her short and dreadful life.

She was still like that when, hours later it seemed, she heard the key in the door, and a sweet, fragrant, only-too-brief draught of the outside air she had feared never to breathe again reached her. Then the two men had secured the door behind them, and came slowly to her.

Now, she thought, close to tears with relief, they would tell her she was free. She would be taken out, blindfolded again most probably, maybe even bound (that she could endure, if she had to) and taken safely back to Pembridge.

But even before he spoke she realised from the Captain's face that this was not to be. He held a folded paper, too thin to contain any enclosure.

'Your uncle wants time,' he said sharply. 'The money was not there.'

CHAPTER
FOUR

FOR a moment or two Deborah stood staring at him, white-faced, her eyes contrastingly wide and black. Slowly, the full significance of what he had said reached her. It was not over. She would not go free. The moment of leaving this horrible place had receded out of reach, indefinitely perhaps. There would be more cold hours, cold days, to pass here, with only her captors for company; there would be more dreadful haunted nights dragging past while she waited alone in the fear that she would be immured there for ever.

She turned from him and fell on the hard little bed, the sobs tearing at her in anguish and despair.

It was more than the Captain, who had not expected so extreme a reaction, could stand.

'Come now, child, it's not the end of the world.' Again there was that note of impatience which reached her, though his words made no sense. 'It may well take him a day or two to gather so much cash, but no more than that. You'll go free very soon—come now, don't weep like that——'

But she could take no comfort. The long strain of the past hours had found its moment of release, and she could not have ceased if she had wished to. Once the Captain touched her tentatively on the shoulder, but the sobbing only grew fiercer. In the end he shrugged, cast a wry glance in Sim's direction, and left her.

Much later, quiet at last, exhausted and empty of emotion, Deborah turned on her side and fell asleep.

It was not a long sleep, for by now her fear and

unhappiness were too great to let her rest. Without that extended bout of crying she would not have slept at all.

When she opened her eyes and looked about her, dully and without interest, she found that the room looked much as it had yesterday, except that it was earlier in the day, and the light was barely sufficient to show her the two sleeping figures on the floor. But today she had no interest at all in studying them, for they served only to remind her of what she had still to endure.

The days, if they passed like yesterday, would not be more than she could bear. Her prison was damp and cold and dismal, but she had to admit even now that the Captain had done his best to make her captivity pass as easily as it could. But the thought of even one more night during which she would have to wait here alone for them to return, was horrible. Her mind began to run over the events of last night again, the panic and terror, the ghastliness of the fear that she might be here for ever.

She pressed her hands over her face, trying to shut out the memory, but it seemed only to bring it more vividly to her mind. The worst thing of all was that she knew there would be no escape, that she would have to go through it all again. And she did not think she could bear it even once more.

When the men awoke their talk, matter-of-fact and mundane, helped a little to distract her. But for all that it was a long day, during which even the meals at which she picked without enthusiasm failed to divert her from the haunting shadow of the approaching night. She wished fervently that there was some way of falling deeply into unconsciousness and waking only when the worst was over, to find the Captain coming triumphantly down the steps with the ransom heavy on his arm.

It was a long day, but the dark came all too soon, and the moment when the men began to make ready to go. It was then that Deborah knew that nothing on earth would make her endure another night like the last.

'Please don't go,' she said at first, her voice faint and pathetic. The Captain turned on his way to the door, surprised.

'Why ever not? The money may well be there tonight.'

She felt her heart gather pace with fear.

'Then let me come with you.' Her voice still did not hold the full weight of her terror, and the Captain smiled.

'We can't do that. After all, it would never do if they took you back without payment, would it?'

'But you don't both need to go——'

'What then if there is a company of soldiers waiting for us? One man would be useless then.'

'So,' she thought, 'would two. And what then?'

She could stand it no more: dignity and self control left her completely. She flung herself on the floor before the Captain, clutching his knees and crying out, 'For the love of God, don't leave me here alone! Take me with you!'

Firmly but gently, the Captain bent and tried to remove her clasp from his legs.

'Don't be foolish, child,' he said sharply. 'We shan't be long. I have a lucky feeling about tonight.'

She began to cry and shout, dragging at his legs, calling almost incoherently for him to take pity on her. At that his patience gave way: calling Sim to help him he hauled her kicking and screaming to the bed and laid her there.

'If you're not quiet I'll tie you to the bed!'

The threat stilled her, though it did not calm her. She crouched on elbows and knees on the bed with her arms closely looped about her head, shutting out as much as she could of sight and sound. But she heard their departing footsteps and the door closing, and the key turning in the lock. Then there was nothing left to do but to wait.

They came back at last, and she knew at once by their silence and the slowness of their steps as they passed through the door that it had not been her last night here. Once more there had been no ransom left, no one to meet them; and this time no letter either. Deborah began to cry, quietly and hopelessly. The Captain made no move to comfort her. His own disappointment, coupled perhaps with his irritation at her behaviour earlier this evening, seemed to have driven all sympathy from him. This time the men ignored her, as if they thought it the best way to bring round a troublesome child, and she lay watching them as they made ready to sleep. Once the light was out, and the darkness stirring with their breathing, she did not close her eyes, but tried to think calmly and without panic.

She knew, with utter conviction, that if she spent another night here alone she would go mad. So far the men had evaded capture, though the dragoons they had spoken of must know the place appointed for the rendezvous. Presumably only their own skill and caution had protected them. But surely it could not last much longer. However incompetent the soldiers, the commanding officer must surely realise very soon that he had only to keep watch throughout the night at the Crooked Oak, and he would have his man. Possibly they feared that she would suffer if they were not able to achieve a complete surprise; but it did not seem likely that they would hold back much longer.

And if they were taken, would the Captain or Sim disclose her whereabouts? Surely not, for that would be to admit their own guilt. So she would starve here, slowly and horribly.

But not, she thought with a sudden new alertness, if she could somehow escape first.

Until that morning in the wood—it seemed a lifetime ago—she had never been allowed to make her own choices, or encouraged to be independent. But now, here in this prison, she had only herself to turn to for help of any kind. And so, having decided what she must do, she set herself to work out, calmly and methodically, how to set about it.

From any angle it looked impossible, but desperation gave her the will to try any means she could think of, however unlikely it was to succeed.

She eliminated first the thought of making any attempt at night, because if, as she suspected, her prison was deep in the woods, she might well lose her way completely in the dark. In any case, she knew from her examination of the room two nights ago that there was no way of escape once the door was locked.

That then left her with no other hope but to leave by the door. She might, perhaps, be able to force her way out when the Captain had it open, for example to let Sim through. But she quickly rejected the idea, for the time being at least. If all else failed she might try it; but she had seen how watchful they were, how cautious, while the door was open, and for how very short a time it *was* ever opened.

In that case she must somehow possess herself of the key and let herself out, locking the door behind her so they could not pursue her. In the dark that would have been difficult enough, and she wondered if it were possible at all in daylight. But she must try, for it offered her one real hope of escape.

She tried to remember first where she had seen the Captain put the key, once he had locked the door. Several minutes of concentration convinced her that it was concealed somewhere about his person, but that was as far as it went. She could not spend precious time, and risk discovery, by setting out to search him—it would, she suspected, be difficult enough to take it even if she knew exactly where he kept it. So before she made her escape she must first watch to see where it was hidden.

Her next step must be to take it, and most likely that could best be done while both men were sleeping. That, undoubtedly, would be the hardest part: she might even have to wait until dark to accomplish it, which would mean risking another night here alone, and having to make her escape at first light tomorrow. She hoped it would not come to that.

Her plan made, Deborah lay quietly waiting for the dawn and, amazingly, found that her new peace of mind, now that the decision was made, lulled her gently into a deep and refreshing sleep.

The first part of the plan went very smoothly, for she woke just as the Captain was letting Sim out to see to the horses. She lay watching him intently from under half-closed lids as he re-locked the door and turned away from it to face her. As he made his way slowly down the steps he slid the key neatly and quickly into the right-hand pocket of his breeches. It was as simple as that.

She had difficulty in concealing her delight, trying to force her features to their former expression of withdrawn melancholy. Fortunately excitement gave her little appetite for breakfast when it came, so that at least helped to allay suspicion.

For the rest of the morning there was no new development which might help her. It was not until late in the afternoon, just when she was beginning to think with a sinking heart that she would have to wait until after the night's long vigil, that an opportunity arose quite unexpectedly.

It was the first time that day that she had not given her full attention to what the men were saying and doing, so she did not realise that Sim was leaving them earlier than usual until he was halfway to the door.

'It's unwise always to come and go at the same time of day,' the Captain explained in answer to her unspoken question, as he came from locking the door. 'It makes it easier for the inquisitive to discover one's actions.'

She said nothing: she had tried as far as possible to imitate the depressed and uncommunicative manner of yesterday in her dealings with the two men. But she was alert again, watching unobtrusively for any opportunity. Not that she expected one, but it would be foolish to miss her chance through inattentiveness.

It was as if fate was playing into her hands today. She had never known it happen before, for except at night there was always one of the men awake and watchful. But this time as they sat there in silence, she half-lying on her bed, he seated at the table, the Captain's head began slowly to droop, nodding and jerking up, then nodding again, until at last it rested on his outstretched arms across the table-top and he was fast asleep.

For a moment or two Deborah could scarcely believe her good fortune. The pocket in which he had placed the key faced her invitingly, just a few feet away. Even if he had been awake she might almost have been able to snatch it before he knew what was happening. But she was not going to risk losing everything by a moment's carelessness. She waited a little longer, then shifted slightly on the bed, and gently tapped her feet on the floor. The Captain did not stir. His head was turned away so she could not see his face, but only the shining hair falling round him on the scarred wood. He was

breathing deeply and quietly, the even breathing of a
man sound asleep.

Very quietly, scarcely daring to breathe herself,
Deborah stood up and then moved step by step towards
the sleeping man. At his side she stopped and looked
down at him, judging the exact movement necessary to
take the key. Then she reached swiftly down and there,
incredibly, easily, the key lay safe in her hand.

The Captain did not move.

There was no time to waste now in triumph if she was
to be gone before dark, and before he woke. She ran
lightly with all the eager speed of excitement up the
steps to the door, and thrust the key into the lock.
Slowly, stiffly, it turned under her hand.

And then at the moment of escape another hand
clasped hers from behind, and all her strength could not
force the key on against the power of the Captain's grip.
It returned inexorably, back the way it had come, and
then was forced from her hand. She had failed.

But she did not know it at once. She turned furiously,
struggling with him for the key. If he had not been still
only half awake he would have overcome her sooner: as
it was she kicked and scratched and bit like a fury for
her freedom, and sent him at last stumbling backwards
down the steps.

He righted himself quickly, and he had the key still,
and Deborah knew that her triumph had been a very
little one. She stood at the door, which was once more
adamantly locked against her, her coif fallen from her
head, her clothes disarrayed, her eyes wide and bright
with unshed tears, expecting his anger and wanting
only to weep as pride would not let her this time.

It was then that she became aware of something
strange and new in the Captain's expression. He stood
motionless and silent at the foot of the steps, and there
was neither anger nor anything else she could recognise

in his eyes. Oddly, the strangeness of it made the colour rise in her face.

Whatever else Deborah saw in his expression, there was certainly surprise. He had risen to his feet from his fall and looked up expecting to see the frightened girl—little more than a child—whom he had so greatly wronged, looking down at him with the despairing primness which should have wrung his heart and troubled his conscience, if he had not silenced it long ago. And instead he found himself gazing at quite another person, not a child but a woman.

Small and slight, certainly, but the slim waist and firm breasts were not those of a child, and the pale unremarkable face had come suddenly alive, framed now in that extraordinary hair, tumbling black and curling and springing with life to her waist, somehow emphasising the delicate fullness of her parted lips, the neat perfection of her nose, the shining darkness of her lovely eyes beneath the finely arched brows. The prim little Puritan had suddenly, amazingly, burst into flower, and the astonishment of the man who saw it was clear in his eyes.

For a long time he gazed at her, the surprise giving place entirely to that unreadable, disquieting something which was so new to Deborah. It troubled and puzzled her, but at last she gave up the attempt to understand and bent to retrieve her coif. There seemed to be a leaden weight somewhere about her middle, heavy and immovable, though the tears had retreated a little before his strangeness. She raised the cap to her head, and his voice broke in: 'Don't——!'

She looked up sharply, astonished at his vehemence. He smiled unsteadily.

'Just as you wish—but you have pretty hair.'

His voice sounded strained and breathless and harsh with whatever emotion lay behind it. Deborah hesitated, and then let her hands fall to her side. After all, she was very much more comfortable without it. She came slowly down the steps towards him, and with an effort—almost visible—he shook off his disturbing mood.

'That was very foolish,' he commented lightly, guiding her back to the bed, his hand on her elbow. 'I might have been compelled to hurt you. Never do it again.'

She sat down, watching him a little bemusedly, as if she were dazed by the loss of her hopes.

'In any case,' he went on, 'it was all unnecessary. All you need is patience: your uncle will bring the money in time.'

She shook her head, the tears flowing swiftly back.

'No,' she said desperately. 'I can't bear to be left alone again.'

'But we always leave you a light,' he objected.

'I know. But what if you were taken? Or killed? What would become of me then?'

Understanding lit his eyes.

'So that's it! I see!' He paused, watching her thoughtfully, and she saw that some new idea had struck him. 'I think perhaps we can use that—your uncle, now—it would move him, would it not, to learn of your fear? What is more, he would realise that if the soldiers took me or Sim, he would have no hope of seeing you again, because you can be sure the secret of this place would die with us ...'

He hesitated at her involuntary cry of dismay, and then went on with uncaring enthusiasm, 'You shall write to him, to tell him what you fear, and then we shall see—it's just what we need to hasten matters.'

She could not take her eyes from him, full as he was of his idea, eager to carry it out, apparently wholly unconcerned at the chilling horror which had given him his opportunity. What kind of man was he, who could so coolly make use of her unhappiness?

Her chief emotion as she watched him was not fear or dismay or disgust, though all were there, but anger, a smouldering fury at his callousness. She raised her head and the angry words were ready on her lips, to tell him exactly what she thought. And then the sound of Sim at the door broke in on her thoughts, and drove them from her mind.

CHAPTER
FIVE

SIM closed the door behind him and stood gazing dourly at them before coming slowly down the steps. The gloom he brought with him enveloped and followed him and spread itself about the little prison. But he said nothing, giving no more acknowledgement of their presence than a curt nod of the head. Instead he lit the candle as it was growing dark, and began to set the night's supper on the table: a sparse one tonight, bread and ale only. Sensing his mood, the Captain broke in, 'Sim, what's behind that long face? Come now, man.'

Sim sat down heavily at the table, and looked up at the Captain. 'I've no good news for you tonight,' he said grimly.

The Captain in his turn pulled a stool to the table and sat down.

'Out with it, Sim. What's to do?'

'I went to Sally Alsop's alehouse at Pembridge tonight, Captain. There was one of the servants from the Hall there, well lost in liquor. He was shouting to the lot of them what the folks at the Hall were doing about the girl's capture. And I didn't like what I heard, not one bit.'

Deborah could see that the Captain was striving not to interrupt again, impatient though he was for Sim to finish his drawn-out story. Sim, making the most of it, poured himself some ale and took several long gulps.

'Well,' he continued at last, wiping the back of his hand across his mouth, 'he said Master Foster did not mean to hand over a penny for the girl's return. He'd

been heard to say more than once that he wasn't
making a pact with rogues. He's called in the dragoons,
and he's dragging things out to give them time to find
you and catch you red-handed with the girl. He sees
himself as a right-thinking man helping to clear the
countryside of vermin.'

'And what,' asked the Captain, his mouth set in a
grim line, 'of my threat to kill her?'

Sim glanced uncomfortably at Deborah, and his
answer was barely audible.

'He has been heard to say—this is what they told me,
mark you, I can't judge the truth of it—but they say he
would rather lose his niece than aid men like you.
"What's one life," he's said to declare, "against the
good of us all?".'

There was a long silence. Deborah sat with head bent
and hands clasped, feeling a little sick. And yet really
she was not surprised: she could almost hear her uncle
declaiming the words.

When she raised her head at last her eyes met those of
the two men, both watching her intently. She was
suddenly afraid. 'What will you do?' she asked in a
whisper, with a little shiver.

'I don't know,' responded the Captain. There was a
dry note in his voice.

There was no trace now in either of them of the
warmth of a few minutes ago. After a moment, the
Captain asked sharply: 'Who inherits if you die?'

For a moment Deborah was startled at the question,
and then, chillingly, she understood. She did not want
to understand, and she answered slowly and reluctantly, as if she could somehow deny the truth of what
she was admitting.

'My uncle,' she said.

The Captain said nothing, but simply continued to
gaze at her. She shivered. It was as if he were saying,

clearly and distinctly, 'Now you see why he will not pay. Very few will blame him for his courageous stand; but I have threatened to kill you, and if you die because he does not hand over the money, then he becomes overnight a rich man. He will pretend when he sees me hang that he is taking a delighted revenge, but in reality he will have used me to gain his own ends. When I took you I played right into his hands.'

Deborah shook her head.

'No,' she said quickly. 'No, it can't be right, what you are thinking. They would not let that happen. Please don't let me think that.'

He stood up.

'I may be wrong,' he said, though his tone belied his words. 'Servants' talk is not always to be trusted. Perhaps the money will be there tonight——'

At that the anger flared up in her.

'Money, always money! Can you think of nothing else? Is that all anyone cares for? It is my life, and my happiness you are all playing with, and no one seems to think of that at all. What use is money? Honest work will give you enough to eat and drink, why should you want more? What in God's name can it bring you that you really need? Happiness, freedom, peace of mind, a clear conscience? Love? You can buy none of these things—I should know, if anyone does. It is nothing, nothing at all. And yet men will kill for it, and steal and hate and plot. What kind of creatures are you that you can be so enslaved? I can only——'

His voice broke in sharply on her words.

'But it is not for me,' he said fiercely, 'I would not do this for myself.'

For a moment the assertion silenced Deborah. She gazed up at him in astonishment.

'Then why?' she asked slowly. 'What possible use can you have for it?'

'I have none, but the King's cause has every need. The King and all those who serve him live in the most abject poverty. Here in England there are stories of luxury and high living. It is all wrong, I tell you. I have seen it, I know. Not one of the King's court but is deep in debt—not because of gaming or extravagance, but simply because they would not otherwise be able to eat. Imagine, if you can, the rightful King of England close to starving, begging for his bread, while men like Sir Edward Biddulph live on the fat of the land and wed themselves to fortunes.'

'And what has Sir Edward ever done to you, that you should be so angry against him?' she retorted.

He hesitated for a moment before replying. 'I could tell you if I wished,' he said quietly, and then added, 'But he is after all typical of his kind, a man without loyalty, feasting while his King starves.'

'Can you only think of men as loyal if they serve your king? What of those like my father, who gave their lives for what they believed to be the good cause, and who would not admit that Charles Stuart had any right to claim the name of King?'

'Whatever they think, however misguided they are, he is their King still, by divine right. And for that I will serve him as long as there is breath in my body.'

'By robbery and murder? I think I would rather have nothing than eat bread gained by such means.'

'But then you, Mistress Halsey,' he said with a glitter of anger in his eyes, 'have never starved.'

Perhaps, she thought, there are other ways of starving than just from lack of food. But she said nothing for a moment, and then asked pointedly:

'And how many innocent victims have died to keep your King fed? How many did you murder before you chose me as your prey?'

'My hands are clean of innocent blood,' he said

grimly. 'What kind of monster do you think I am?'

I know now, thought that detached part of herself, what has made you what you are. Or I think I do—passion for a cause, hatred of its enemies, defeat and desperation. What, she wondered, had he been before all this ruled his life? Perhaps Sir Edward was right not to be swayed too much by an ideal, not to let a principle blind him to the humanity of those who did not share his views. But then she suspected that Sir Edward was hardly a shining example of compassion and understanding. She felt tired suddenly, bleakly aware of her own loneliness, of the lack of hope which faced her on every side. She raised her eyes sadly to the Captain's face.

'You would have killed me,' she reminded him quietly, answering his question at last. 'Perhaps you will still.' Somehow it did not seem to matter much at the moment. 'But why me? What have I done to be chosen as your victim?—No,' she went on before he could speak, 'I know of course. I am a Puritan and an heiress. That was all you needed.'

'And,' he went on slowly, 'because you were betrothed to Sir Edward Biddulph.'

She frowned, puzzled at his again bringing up that name.

'I don't understand that. What have you to do with him?'

'Nothing, now. But once, many years ago, he did me, and others, a great wrong. For that I can never forgive him. For that I would do all in my power to hurt him. In taking you I sought to help the King's cause, but also to have my revenge, to make him suffer.'

'And do you suppose that he does suffer?' she asked. 'Do you think he cares at all that I am in your power?'

'I imagine he has no wish to lose a part of your fortune before he has laid hands on it,' he said cynically.

'I suppose it might even grieve him a little to think that his future wife was in a position of some danger. Who knows, he may even rejoice when he has you safely home.'

'That, then,' said Deborah slowly, after a moment, 'is why you threatened to throw my body in Sandwell mere. I wondered once or twice why you did not choose the pond at Pembridge, close to my uncle's house. But it was not my uncle you really wished to hurt.'

A note of exasperation crept into her voice. 'But it is all so stupid! What point was there in having your revenge? I am sure my death, or the humiliation of Sir Edward, would put nothing right for you. Would you have been satisfied once the waters closed over my head?'

For a moment he hesitated, and she was aware of some emotion flickering briefly in the darkness of his eyes. But he only said lightly:

'Revenge is sweet,' and turned away from her to the table.

She sat for a long time gazing at her hands, trying to accept the new situation which faced her. How could she believe, against all common sense and natural feeling, that her uncle wished her dead, that he could wish for anything but her well-being? It was preposterous. And yet—what was that Nan had said, asserting that her aunt's harshness stemmed as much from jealousy as moral fervour? Had Nan been right? If so, then the rest could so easily be true—and somewhere inside her lurked a disturbing, uneasy conviction that the Captain had seen only too clearly where the truth lay.

She had accepted that they did not love her; but until now she had always taken it for granted that they cared for her well-being and would not actively wish her harm. If the Captain was right, it left her without protection or security or anything but the force of her own character between herself and the worst that life could do to her. Nan, her one friend, was as vulnerable as herself.

She shivered a little, and then looked up at the man who had brought her to this. He was watching her intently, almost as if he read her thoughts, and she could not decipher the expression in his sombre eyes. There was no softness in them, no comfort, yet there was no hatred either. She gazed back at him, full of a sense of her own helplessness.

Sim's voice broke in on their silence.

'Are you going to sup tonight, Captain? It's high time to go for the money.'

The Captain looked round sharply.

'The money? But you said the uncle would not pay it.'

'That's what they said, but who's to say it's right? There'd be no sense in missing it through not looking, this once at least. Maybe tomorrow, if it's not there, we can think what's to be done——'

The Captain was silent for a moment, lost in thought, and then broke in:

'No, I've a better idea. We'll try what the letter will do.'

'The letter, Captain?' asked a bewildered Sim.

'Yes,' said the Captain. 'A letter from Mistress Halsey fit to wring the heart of all but the most relentless of uncles. Imploring in piteous terms for him to rescue her from her plight—is that right, Mistress Halsey?' he turned, half-smiling, and seeing she was about to speak went on more pleasantly: 'At least it would be one way to find out if they put you before your fortune.'

She hated him for remembering his scheme to make use of her fear; yet he was right. If the letter moved her uncle, she would know she was not entirely friendless.

But what if it did not? She shivered. It was bad enough to doubt, to fear that the Captain was right, but to know, without any possible remaining uncertainty, that her uncle wished her dead—where would that leave her then? She shook her head fiercely.

'No, I'll not write. You can't make me do that!'

'No?' asked the Captain. 'I can make you do exactly as I please—pen and paper and ink, Sim—and you come to the table, Mistress Halsey.'

She sat rigid on the bed, her hands clasped on her lap, defying him in silence. His eyes narrowed.

'Don't anger me, sweeting,' he said very softly.

'Sweeting.' He had called her that once before. She could not remember that anyone had ever in all her life addressed her with any term of endearment. And now he used that word, which should have been full of tenderness and love, and it was loaded only with menace. She rose very slowly and took her seat at the table, and he relaxed a little.

'That's better.' He took the writing materials from Sim and laid them before her. 'Now, can you find the words, or shall I tell you what to say?'

She was trembling, close to tears.

'I . . . I don't know . . .' she said. She made no move to write.

He raised the quill and his slender fingers forced open her hand and closed it around the pen. He drew the ink nearer to her.

'Then write what I say: "My dear uncle"—is that how you'd begin?'

'No!' she said, shuddering at the disrespect. 'He would be in a fury at the discourtesy.'

He watched her with his head on one side, a brief ironic smile twisting his lips. Then he tried again.

'What about "respected sir"? Or "honourable sir"?'

'"Most honoured uncle",' she decided, and began to

write. But after 'uncle' she paused again, unable even to begin to say what she felt. The Captain intervened smoothly, delivering the frightened imploring phrases without emotion.

'"I am alone and in danger of my life, without hope or comfort,"' he dictated. '"Sometimes I am left alone in this place for hours together, and I think I shall lose my reason. If you take my captors prisoner, sir, then I shall be lost for ever; for only they know where I am, and if they are taken they will never talk. Then I shall die in this dark place and you will never see me again. I beg you by the love there was between my dear mother and my aunt your wife, by every Christian feeling, that you will pay what they ask and set me free; and that soon, or you may find that I come back to you a mindless idiot, crazed by fear and horror.

'"I am, sir, your unhappy but dutiful niece,

Deborah Halsey."'

As she signed her name the Captain reached over to take the letter, folding it neatly, and she bent her head on her arms in despair that he could know so well what she felt and yet not wish to comfort her.

'I'll take it, Captain,' she heard Sim say, his voice full of eagerness for the errand. 'You'll want it to go right to Pembridge, I suppose?'

The Captain gave his instructions, and then she heard the retreating footsteps mounting the stairs, the door opening and closing. When she looked up at last she was once more alone with the man who had brought her to this.

CHAPTER
SIX

THE CAPTAIN stood watching her, and their eyes met as Deborah raised her head. She was struck again, with that strange lurch of the stomach, by his beauty. Dark long-lashed eyes, full of unfathomable thoughts; fine dark brows; the fair, perfect features; the hair shining pale gold in the candlelight; the flawless curve of jaw and cheekbone; the tall lithe grace of the body, the assured poise of the head, the beautiful slender hands. And the coolness, the calm line of the mouth, the untroubled gaze. As if his conscience were clear and everything going exactly according to plan.

It was then that a burning anger enveloped her: she had never before been so swept out of herself with fury, her eyes blazing, brilliantly dark, her face glowing. She rose to her feet and confronted him, her hand clutching the edge of the table as if only that kept her from flinging herself on him to tear him to pieces.

'I have never in all my life hated a single human being,' she said, 'but you I hate with everything there is in me. You talk of your cause and your King, you say you are not guilty of innocent blood, yet you can look on the misery of a woman who has done you no possible harm and see only that it can be of use to you. I hate you, but even more I despise you. You are not worthy of love or respect or loyalty. God knows why Sim stays with you—if I were him I'd have given you up to the soldiers long since, and made sure I was well rewarded for it. Whatever my uncle thinks of me, whatever Sir Edward did to you once, you are not even worthy of their hatred. You are less than nothing, a man without honour, or principle, or anything else worthy of the name of man!'

She knew her words had struck home. Triumphantly, she saw the colour rise in his face, the amazement in his eyes, and when he spoke there was no assurance in his abrupt words.

'But what would you have?—Only my wits stand between me and death—Mistress Halsey, if I did not use what life offers me, then I could not live.'

'I think,' she said with utter scorn, 'that I would rather die than live as you do, preserving my cowardly skin by means of the misery of others.'

She swung sharply away from him to make her way to the bed, but halfway there his hand grasped her shoulder and drew her back to face him. He held her so, his eyes on hers, and again there was that unreadable expression, and with it something more. Shame? Surely not; yet she knew she had moved him somehow. And for this moment at least she was not afraid, for the anger had driven out every trace of fear. Her head was high, her eyes defiantly returning his gaze.

And then, suddenly, totally without warning, she was drawn into his arms, held ruthlessly, harshly, and before she could cry out she was silenced irrevocably by the force of his mouth on hers, crushing her lips with a relentless passion which took her breath away. She struggled angrily but uselessly against the strength of his grasp, trying desperately to free herself.

Then she felt one hand make its way caressingly down her back, the other twisting in the thickness of her hair, his mouth move to the slender line of her throat above the soiled collar, and a new and disturbing sensation drove out her anger. The room swam about her, hazed and darkened, as if only his nearness was real, the lithe muscular strength of his body, the warmth of his lips on her skin. Her struggling ceased, her body stilled, and with no will left of her own her arms crept up as if to clasp him, her being melted to nothingness, merged into his. There had been no moment like this in all her life, no sweetness so sharp and so fiercely intoxicating.

And then as suddenly, equally without warning, he let her go, drawing sharply away, breathless, sombre of expression.

'Damn you!' was all he said, with a harshness which shocked her, trembling still from his embrace. He turned to the table and poured ale and gulped it down without pausing, and then began to pace the room at the far side.

'Get yourself some supper and to bed!' he flung across the table at her.

She did not move, bewildered by his abrupt change of mood, this new harshness which lacked all the coolness and reserve of before. What had she done? Why had her moment of anger affected him so strangely? What had happened between them just now?

'Take your eyes off me, woman, and do as I say!'

Frightened, she grabbed bread and ale from the table and took it to her bed. She had no appetite at all, but forced herself to eat and drink a little, watching him furtively, anxiously, until his eyes met hers and flashed with anger. Then she turned away and rolled herself in the blanket, and made a hopeless attempt to sleep.

He was still pacing the room when Sim returned, though he stopped then, and she heard the servant recounting how he had delivered the letter, unobserved, to Pembridge.

'One nasty moment, I had,' the man added. 'I sighted the soldiers just the other side of Pembridge crossroads, and I was hard put to it to give them the slip. Had to come a long way round through the woods...'

'Yes, yes,' she heard the Captain respond impatiently, 'but it doesn't matter now——— What time is it? Is it daybreak yet?'

'Just on the turn, I'd say,' Sim replied, a slightly puzzled note in his voice, as if even he was aware of something strange in his master's mood.

'Have you unsaddled your horse?'

'Of course, Captain.'

'Then saddle her up again, and mine too—Don't stand there gawping, do as I say!'

At that Deborah rolled over, her eyes wide open, her heart lurching. Were they going to leave her alone again?

'But it's nearly light, Captain———' Sim was beginning to protest, until he caught sight of the Captain's expression. 'Yes, Captain, I'll go at once.'

Deborah sat up, ready to plead with them not to leave her; but before she could speak the Captain was making his way towards her.

'Get up, you're coming with us.'

She gasped, her hand to her mouth.

'Coming with you! But why? Where to?'

'Don't ask questions, just come.'

She was trembling, caught between fear and elation, as she scrambled to her feet and pulled her cloak about her. To leave this place, to go out into the air, to see the grass and the trees and the sky as she had feared she might never do again———! But where was he taking her? What might her anger have driven him to?

He grasped her wrist and drew her to his side, and bound her arms. And then he untied his silken sash to tie it about her eyes. So she would not see the grass after all.

She stood quietly until he was ready, and then allowed him to lead her up the steps to the door and out into the air.

She could not see where she was, but she could feel it, and the sweet cold freshness of the air was so intoxicating, so unexpectedly delightful, after her long incarceration that for a moment Deborah paused, her misery forgotten, and stood breathing in the reviving fragrance. Then the Captain pulled at her elbow, and she allowed him to lead her over the uneven ground.

She could hear the horses stamping and snorting, and smell their warm pungency. Somewhere a bird was singing, and a little breeze sprung up. Even this little moment of freedom, whatever might come, was unbearably sweet.

Whatever the Captain planned, she knew that Sim was not in agreement, for she heard him muttering and grumbling as he brought the horses to meet them.

'Be quiet, Sim, you fool,' said the Captain sharply. She felt him move away from her, and heard the creak of the harness as he swung himself into the saddle, and then Sim grasped her from behind and raised her, and the Captain reached down to help her on to the saddle before him. His arm held her firmly against him, and she had a moment's disturbing recollection of what had happened earlier that night in the prison. But there was no hint of passion now in his grasp.

She heard Sim mount his own horse, and in a low voice the Captain gave the word to move off. The hooves thudded on earth, rattled on that hard surface she remembered from the night of her arrival, moved again on to softer ground.

Then all at once there were other horses moving towards them, many of them, hooves thundering closer.

Behind her the Captain swore, and shouted to Sim: 'Into the trees!' and their mounts swung into a gallop, labouring uphill, the intruders in close pursuit. They reached the trees at last, for low branches caught at them, forcing them to slow, winding their way to find a path. The pursuers were closer, though still in the open: there was a confused noise of horses, voices shouting, jingling harness.

Then more horses, in front of them this time, and from the side. Another horse—Sim's it seemed—backed against them. She felt the Captain pull out his pistol and fire, the sound harsh, sharp, at her ear. A shot answered it, and another, and then their own horse reared, pawing the air and with a long horrible scream stumbled to the ground.

Hands were on her then, dragging and pulling at her from all sides. She cried out and they carried her struggling beyond the reach of the mêlée and threw her to the ground. The rope at her wrists had come loose, and she freed her hands and reached up and tore the sash from her eyes. The low slanting dawn sunlight dazzled her in its brilliance, needling its way through the golden trees.

There, a short way off, the breastplates and helmets of the dragoons gleamed in the sunlight, and in the midst of them the Captain stood with Sim's fallen body at his feet, backed against a tree with his sword in his hand. There was an undeniable splendour about him, standing there with the sun on his shining hair and the soldiers closing in on him, with only his sword between himself and capture. She watched as the blade flashed out everywhere, darting, nimble, holding them off for a moment longer. Then she lost sight of him behind the encroaching band of soldiers, and she knew they had him. She was free, and she was safe at last. Overwhelmed with relief, she buried her face in her hands.

Someone touched her shoulder.

'Mistress Halsey?' A brisk, businesslike tone. She

raised her head and nodded at the officer, lost for words.

'You're safe now. We've got him. Soon have you safe home.'

And she went with him towards the waiting troop.

CHAPTER
SEVEN

DEBORAH knew she should be elated now, ready to sing for joy at her freedom, to shout to the world her satisfaction at the capture of that hated man. She should at least have been full of warm thanks to the dragoons for their timely rescue.

Instead she could think of nothing to say at all. She felt numbed, depressed, empty of feeling and emotion. She allowed them to lead her to a horse, to help her to mount; she waited while the soldiers assembled for the march and watched as the prisoner, relentlessly bound, was led to his place just a few paces in front of her. Then the order was given to move and the horses urged forward, and they were on their way.

From time to time the Captain of the dragoons who rode at her side addressed some remark to her in a kindly tone; but she did not hear what he said, and merely responded with a non-committal murmur. She knew she was being discourteous, but she could do no more. After a while the officer gave up the attempt to demonstrate his concern for the girl he had so successfully rescued, and relapsed into silence, concluding that she was too shaken by her recent experience for idle conversation.

She did not notice anything about the route they took, though she was dimly aware of the trees all about her, red and gold and bronze in the filtered sunlight. Perhaps because of all the wrongs he had done her, she was more conscious by far of the man in front. He had a red stain on his torn sleeve where, she supposed, a bullet had grazed him, and the dragoons were moving at a pace just a little too fast for him, though he showed no sign of weariness, as far as she could see.

Then the woods drew back, and they were on the road; and a little further on they came to a crossroads which at last she recognised, where the track divided for Sandwell and Pembridge, and the main road led on until in the end it would come to London. Here the officer at her side gave the order to halt, and the small company came to a noisy clattering standstill.

'Lieutenant Lofthouse here will escort you home, Mistress Halsey,' said her companion. 'We'll get this fellow to Maidstone and safely behind bars as soon as we can. I'll be along to see how you're doing in a day or two.'

She murmured a brief and courteous farewell as the Lieutenant came to her side. And then, not quite knowing why—almost against her will—she turned once to look at the prisoner before she went on her way, and at that moment he looked round. He was calm, unsmiling, just as she had seen him so often, but something held her gaze, as if there was some message for her in those unfathomable eyes. When the soldiers jerked him back into line and led him away, she should have rejoiced; but she watched him go with an odd emptiness deep inside her, as if in his going he had taken something from her.

'They'll have him hanged as soon as the law allows, don't you fear,' said her escort. She glanced at him sharply, but made no response to his cheerful grin. She felt closer to tears than to smiling, utterly weary as she was.

'Time to get you home,' said the Lieutenant kindly, reaching over to take her horse's rein and turn it along the road to Pembridge. He meant well, Deborah knew, but she had a great hunger to be quiet and alone, and that was obviously very far from the Lieutenant's mind. He was a short square-set man, showing signs of a healthy masculine interest in the dishevelled but undoubtedly very lovely girl he was escorting home. And she, he felt, showed a depressing lack of gratitude for her rescue, and no interest at all in this particular individual who had played a part in that rescue. She paid only the barest attention to his remarks and showed no sign that she had even noticed him. But then she had suffered several days of captivity in the hands of that notorious villain, and goodness only knew what indignities he had inflicted upon her in that time. The Lieutenant's chivalrous blood boiled at the very thought: he felt he would like to have the privilege of hanging the man personally.

As well as being beautiful, the girl was also, he had been told, a substantial heiress. To a bachelor on a soldier's pay that was an interesting piece of information: he would, he thought, make a point of calling to inquire after her now and then, once she had recovered from her ordeal. He remembered that his Captain had indicated his intention to do the same, and decided he had no time to waste in making a favourable impression on his companion—and, if possible, on her relations.

'Disgraceful that a rogue like that should be roaming around the countryside for so long,' he said heartily. 'Pity we weren't called in sooner, then you'd not have had to go through all that.'

She looked round then, her dark eyes wide and unhappy, and he congratulated himself on catching her interest.

'Please don't talk of it,' she said with a shiver.

He tried again, on a more cheerful note.

'Lovely spell of weather, this. That sun will soon put the roses back in your cheeks. Fine garden, have they at Pembridge Hall? I can just imagine you gathering flowers to brighten the house; sitting at your sewing in some sunny corner; talking to your friends as you wander among the orchard trees.' 'I'm getting quite poetical,' he thought with pleasure.

Deborah, who had spent no more time in the garden than was needed to gather an essential herb for her aunt, was unmoved. She gave him a fleeting, wintry smile, which showed that she had heard nothing, and bent her head again so that her face was shaded by her flowing hair. The Lieutenant resisted the temptation to reach across and lay a hand on that lovely hair, and decided that his attempt to win her confidence must wait. Clearly she was in no state to appreciate his finer points at the moment.

In any case he saw, looking up, that they had reached the straggle of houses which constituted the village of Pembridge, and the Hall stood facing them across the green with its duckpond, eggshell blue on this lovely day.

'Here we are,' he said briskly, but she kept her face hidden. 'Poor little thing,' he thought to himself, and quickened his horse's pace to have her home the sooner.

News of her escape had not yet reached the Hall, and they rode along the edge of the green watched curiously by the early risers among the villagers, to find no sign of life at her uncle's house. From the stables came the sounds of jingling harness, and the whistling of a groom going about his work; but they were the only signs of life. The Lieutenant dismounted, reached up to help her to the ground (delightful, to have his hands briefly about her trim waist), and marched up the three shallow steps to hammer on the front door. It was opened a little later by the maid Betty, who looked as if she were troubled at confronting a visitor so early in the morning.

'Anyone awake in there?' asked the Lieutenant

cheerfully. 'Here's Mistress Halsey for you, brought
back safe and sound.'

Betty pushed wide the door and threw up her hands
with a transparent pleasure which astonished Deborah,
and lifted her spirits just a little. The servant peered
round the Lieutenant, to verify the truth of his words,
and smiled at Deborah, and then stood back.

'You'd best come in. I'll go for Master and Mistress.'

She ran lightly away on her errand, and the Lieutenant turned to usher Deborah into the house. She
shivered as she passed through the door, out of the
sunlight into the scrubbed austerity of the hall: fireless,
without picture or ornament, furnished only with
fiercely polished bench and table and a very upright
chair. It was as if chill reality had closed about her
again as she stepped across the threshold, leaving
behind the last few days as if they had all been a dream.
A bad dream; yet she had the odd sense that what she
had come home to was worse than what she had left
behind.

And there in a moment was her aunt, descending the
stairs with unhurried dignity and no trace of eagerness
or gladness. Deborah might just now have returned
from market for all the emotion she showed. She
inclined her head briefly to the Lieutenant as he intro-
duced himself and announced his errand.

'Thank you,' she said coolly. 'Please convey to your
fellows our thanks for taking prisoner that villainous
Captain Black. That is one scourge the less to trouble
us. Betty will show you the way to the kitchen, where
you may break your fast.'

Lieutenant Lofthouse realised that he was being
dismissed, before he had found any opportunity to
make himself pleasant to the young lady's relations. He
hid his mortification, and attempted a parting shot.

'If I may, I should like to call tomorrow, to see how

Mistress Halsey goes on. Once she has had time to recover a little, that is.'

'Thank you,' said Mistress Foster, unbending, 'but that will not be necessary. Mistress Halsey will not be receiving visitors.'

Reddening slightly, the Lieutenant bowed, and followed Betty towards the kitchen, cheering himself with the reflection that perhaps the heiress was already spoken for, which explained her aunt's clear rebuff. That was his hard luck, but not his fault: there were other fish in the sea, if none which he had so far found quite so enticing.

Aunt Susan watched until he was out of sight, and then turned to Deborah. Still she showed no warmth, no emotion at all, simply a long cool appraisal, which set Deborah's heart beating with anxiety as to what she might have done wrong. It was a familiar sensation, but surely ridiculous in this instant? At this time of all times there could be nothing to evoke her aunt's criticism.

She remembered suddenly the Captain's implied accusation, that her aunt and uncle had wanted her death, and tried to push the thought aside. She was home, and she must be thankful and ready to join in their rejoicing, for surely they must be happy to have her safe.

'How fortunate,' said her aunt eventually, 'that you are home in time for morning prayers. Your uncle will I am sure delay them sufficiently for you to do something about your hair. Where is your coif?'

'I . . . I don't know,' stammered Deborah, colouring a little: until now she had forgotten its existence. She had a brief recollection of descending stone steps by candlelight, the coif in her hand, and the Captain gazing at her with that unreadable light in his eyes. She bent her head, because for some unaccountable reason the memory brought her close to tears. She must wait to weep until she was alone, and then she could sob out all the fear and tension of the past days where no one could see her.

'Go and find another then. And do not keep us waiting any longer than is necessary.'

Deborah set out at a run, and then, at a sharp word from her aunt, slowed to a brisk walk and mounted the stairs to that familiar room. There was no sign of Nan—presumably she had not yet heard of her mistress's return—and everything was immaculately tidy, but tainted with a faint coating of dust. 'They did not expect me then,' she thought, and then was angry at herself for thinking it. The tears so long unshed began to flood her eyes as she bent over the chest at the foot of the bed.

It took her some time to find the coif, with that mistiness clouding her vision, and her hands were trembling too much for her to conceal her hair as well as her aunt would wish. She was dirty, and her clothes torn and grimy, but there was no time for more. They were waiting.

'I must not cry,' she whispered fiercely to herself, and thrust her head high and straightened her back as she left the room.

The entire household was already ranged in the hall when she reached it, silent, watchful, solemn. It was almost as if they welcomed her return not with thankfulness and relief, but with hostility. Even Betty's head was bent, so that she had no kindly glance to meet her eyes. But from the far corner by the window she heard a gasp, and looked up to see Nan standing there, and her joy was clear on her face. But her uncle's voice, intervening swiftly, reminded her of why she was here.

'Deborah, we are waiting,' he said. She took her place at his side, stealing a look at him as she did so. There was no warmth here either, simply sternness and the inevitable sense of duty.

The Bible reading was chosen with care, she noted: the story of the return of the prodigal son. 'Where is my fatted calf, then?' she thought, though she was comforted a little by the possibility that her return meant more to them than their manner suggested. Then her uncle moved on to the prayers: solemn thanks for the bodily preservation of His child, Deborah, and a wish that this might also be a means for her salvation. And then a succession of pleas for her to see the error of her ways, seek forgiveness, and receive conversion. Deborah felt hurt, and a little bewildered, for why should they look on her misfortune as if it were an act of wrongdoing?

The prayers were long, and in the end she ceased to listen, so that she was still standing with bent head when her uncle gave the words of dismissal. Nan, coming eagerly to greet her, was abruptly despatched to the kitchen by Aunt Susan, and Deborah did not look up until she had left the room.

Breakfast now, in the parlour, at the long table where she sat halfway along one side with her aunt at one end and her uncle at the other. It was a long and silent meal, though now and then her uncle would address some insignificant remark to his wife, or she to him, and receive a brief reply. To Deborah they said nothing at all, which perhaps was just as well, as she found she could not eat and had to sit with teeth firmly clenched to prevent herself from crying. In this she was not entirely successful, and in the end her aunt said to her sharply:

'Stop snivelling, girl!'

At that the floodgates opened, and Deborah buried her head on her arms and gave way to uncontrollable weeping, oblivious of the rebukes falling upon her from either side, no longer caring what they thought of her.

After some time her uncle's patience gave way entirely.

'Deborah, go to your room,' he commanded. 'Wait there until your aunt comes to you.'

Deborah fled from the parlour, ignoring their reminders not to run. It was a relief to be alone, to lie stretched out on her bed and cry as much as she wished, quietly and miserably, with a slow desperation for which there seemed to be no reason and no cure.

By the time her aunt came to her she was weeping only at intervals, lying still between whiles with eyes closed, overcome with weariness. She did not move when Mistress Foster came to the bedside, and her aunt was clearly displeased.

'Rise to your feet, girl, when I am in the room. Where are your manners?'

Deborah dragged herself slowly to a sitting position, and swung her legs to the floor. But when she tried to stand she swayed and almost fell, and had to sit down again at once.

'I'm sorry,' she said faintly. 'I think I'm not very well.'

Aunt Susan surveyed her, unmoved, for a moment or two, and then said: 'Very well. You had better get into bed. I will leave what I had to say until tomorrow morning, when you have rested. You will realise, of course, that a great deal has changed, and can never be as it was.'

That, Deborah thought, was only too clear, though she was not quite sure what her aunt meant. She was grateful enough now simply to undress, once Mistress Foster had gone, and crawl between the sheets.

She was exhausted, but she did not sleep other than fitfully, though neither could she think clearly. A succession of images chased each other around her mind, memories of her captivity, distorted, bewildering recollections of the crowding events of this morning.

She tossed restlessly, trying to find some comfort in it all.

And then the door opened, and Nan came in, and she sat up to clasp her maid in her arms, the tears flowing again, but gently now.

'I thought I'd never get away to see how you were,' said Nan. 'The way you looked at prayers gave me quite a turn.' She sat on the bed, and Deborah lay down again. 'How are you, Mistress Deborah? Was it very bad?'

'No,' said Deborah with trembling lips. 'At least, I think it's worse to be back.' She thought as she spoke how foolish that sounded, and yet it was true.

Nan made a wry face.

'I suppose that's some comfort. Do you want to tell me about it?'

How could she even begin, tired as she was? Deborah wondered. 'No,' she said. 'I wish I could sleep. I'm so tired, but there's so much in my head.'

'Then I'll sing to you, like I did when you were a little girl, in trouble for something and lying awake. Would you like that?'

Nan's voice was low and not very tuneful, but it had an undeniably soothing quality. So as not to offend the susceptible members of the household, she selected for performance a number of psalms; but Deborah did not mind what she chose. Listening to her she found her mind calmed, emptied of anxiety, until slowly and gently she fell asleep.

She was alone when she awoke, and it was clearly well into the night, for the house was silent, only an owl hooting somewhere far off in the woods. Into her mind came the thought, unbidden, that this time last night she had been in the arms of Captain Black. She ought to have shivered at the memory, pushed it from her mind, but she did not. She did not even want to.

Instead she lay there remembering every moment of that incident, the feel of his fingers in her hair, his mouth on hers, the strength of his arms, the passion of his kiss. And when she shivered then it was not with fear or horror. She remembered other things too: the candlelight on his hair, the slender hands busy at some task, the fleeting glimpse of a transforming smile, hinting at some gentleness long suppressed.

Her mind moved on, to his odd harshness after he had drawn back from that embrace, a harshness which had been quite different, she knew instinctively, from the ruthlessness of his manner before that time. Then his sudden decision to take her from that place, a decision he had not even explained to Sim. What had he meant to do with her? Would she have ended a short time later drowned in Sandwell Mere, as he had threatened? Surely if that was what he meant to do, he would have killed her before they left the prison?

She would never know, because that decision so suddenly made had brought him to disaster. She remembered him facing his enemies, sword in hand; she thought of him marching a prisoner before her; she thought of him turning to look at her for that moment at the crossroads.

And she knew then that she did not rejoice at his capture, that most of her grief, the large part of her tears, were not for her weariness and her loneliness, but for him.

At that moment in the prison when she had confronted him and flung her hatred in his face, every word she had cried had been a lie. She knew that now. For she had thrown her heart after them, and he had only been putting the seal on her love when he had reached to take her in his arms. She loved him. She knew it now. Wherever he was, whatever might become of him, he had her heart for ever and ever.

She did not pause to wonder if he cared even a little for her, beyond the momentary attraction which had led him to kiss her. For she thought then only of his plight: the man she loved a prisoner, in danger greater than any he had faced before. They would bring him to trial and hang him, and there would be nothing at all she could do to help him. Her new love, deep and strong as it was, could not break through to halt the relentless process of justice.

Or could it?

She sat up suddenly, clasping her knees, her eyes wide and alert in the darkness. Suppose—just suppose—she were to go to Maidstone, to be present at his trial, to stand up in court and cry out that he was not the man they thought him; that he had been kind to her, that he was good, she knew he was good. It did not matter that it was not quite true. She who had never in all her life told the smallest white lie would do that for him, gladly, wholeheartedly. Surely that would move them!

But what if she were to do that and it failed, and they condemned him all the same? The flame died in her, and she bent her head to her knees. She was very young, very inexperienced in the ways of the world. She knew only that she wanted desperately to help, but not what best she could do. What she needed now, she knew, was a friend: a calm kindly, sensible friend who knew the world and would be ready to advise her.

She searched around in her mind for such a person. Nan might know someone, though that seemed unlikely; or perhaps the minister, for he had seemed kind, but she must tread carefully until she was sure. Her whole being shrank at the thought of standing before a judge and declaring that this notorious highwayman had used her kindly, and that she loved him; but that would be a small sacrifice to make for saving his life, if that was what was needed.

That resolution taken, another slowly crystallised in her mind, and to achieve that would, she was quite sure, be very difficult. She would not, under any circumstances, marry Sir Edward Biddulph. Marriage to him had seemed a bleak enough prospect when she had known nothing better; but now she knew that she could not bear it. She knew that love had nothing to do with marriage, except sometimes, if one were fortunate, by chance: marriage was a matter of property and inheritance, and perpetuation of the family name; love was a luxury indulged in only by the poor.

But after those moments in the Captain's arms, after her brief incomparable taste of what love might offer, she knew she could not marry any man but one, and Sir Edward least of all. Not that she was foolish enough to think she could break the engagement easily, for at the least it would be humiliating for Sir Edward, and her uncle and aunt would be furious. If the worst came to the worst, and they would not accept her decision, she would be driven to refuse him at the wedding ceremony itself; but better that than a lifetime bound to him beyond recall.

By the time dawn broke her two resolutions had hardened to an immovable firmness, and she felt ready to fight for them with all the power at her disposal. She debated whether to say anything to Nan, when the maid should come to help her dress, and decided to remain silent for the time being.

But to her surprise it was her aunt who came to her first, and not Nan. Determined to give Aunt Susan every opportunity to show her kinder side, Deborah sat up with a smile and greeted her pleasantly. But her aunt's expression remained dauntingly severe.

'You will dress yourself and come to prayers within fifteen minutes,' she said. 'It is time you cast aside the frivolity of having a servant to wait·on you. All that is over.'

An unaccountable chill crept over Deborah.

'Where's Nan, then?' she asked sharply, as if she had some kind of premonition.

'She has left your service. We have quite enough servants here without her.'

For a moment Deborah was speechless with horror, and then she cried out: 'But you can't do that! She has been with me all my life. Have I no right to say who is to serve me?'

'I hardly think so, now,' said her aunt, unmoved.

'What do you mean, "now"? What has changed so much?' An incredible possibility occurred to her. 'Am I no longer rich? Has the money gone?'

'Not,' said her aunt, 'to my knowledge. But——'

'Then Nan can stay. She will not be a burden on you, but it is my duty and my right to take care of her. I will not have her cast off as if she meant nothing to me.'

'She will doubtless find another position. But as I was about to say when you interrupted me, you surely cannot expect everything to be as it was, after all that has happened.'

'After all what?' asked Deborah in miserable bewilderment. 'I am no different, surely, because I was taken for ransom?' Though she felt her colour rising as she spoke, knowing that she had indeed changed, but she asked herself how her aunt could possibly know that, when she had only just learned it herself.

Her aunt stared at her as if she found such stupidity hard to credit.

'You have just returned to us after passing three days and four nights in the company of a notorious high-wayman,' said Mistress Foster, as if that explained everything. When Deborah continued to gaze at her uncomprehendingly she went on: 'You went to him young and a virgin. You surely cannot expect us to believe that you return with your purity intact?'

Deborah felt a rush of colour to her face, and a furious anger. How dared they imply that she was so weak, and he so without scruples! Even if he had been all they thought him, surely she would be more deserving of pity than of blame?

And then she remembered his arms about her, and the sweetness of that moment when his mouth found hers; and how willing she would have been for him to have taken more, far more; and the irony of it almost drove her to bitter laughter. But not quite.

'Would my word be enough to convince you?' she demanded, her eyes bright and hard.

'Of course not,' said Aunt Susan, oblivious of the fury in Deborah's tone. 'When you came here first,' she went on, 'we were happy to welcome you into our house, as the daughter we never had. We were content that you should be used with all the consideration and love and care which we would have shown to a daughter. So, of course, we humoured your whim by allowing Nan to stay. But now all that has changed, as you must see when you have given thought to the matter. You can no longer be a daughter to us, or in any sense our equal. If it were possible, you would be permitted to sleep with the servants, but I think your example would not be a good one. For the time being you may continue to use this room, but in no other respect will things be as they were. Get that clear in your head, Deborah, or you will find it hard to accept what must be your lot. You are less to us now than the servants, for you have fallen lower than they; but in all charity we would not drive you away, for we still have a duty towards you, as Christians, to bring you to a better path. Get dressed now, I have wasted too much time already. You will break your fast alone in here after prayers.'

She turned to go, and Deborah watched her, appalled. And then she tried one parting shot.

'Aunt Susan, I will not marry Sir Edward.'

Mistress Foster paused, no sign of dismay on her face.

'Of course not,' she said. 'That is out of the question now.'

CHAPTER
EIGHT

Nan had gone without trace. Deborah did not even
know when she had left, but she was not among the
servants at morning prayers. She herself stood alone at
a point halfway between the grouped servants and her
aunt and uncle, a position emphasising her present
isolation; a member of neither group, an individual
without a right to any place. Today she was not even
considered worthy of a mention in the prayers.

It was something of a relief, at least, to be considered
unfit to eat at her uncle's table. A plate and a tankard
were thrust into her hands as she crossed the hall and
she retreated thankfully with them to her room. At
least, she thought, her own company was probably a
good deal more congenial at present than that of anyone else in the house.

But however philosophical she tried to be, there was
very little comfort or humour to be found in her new
circumstances. After breakfast her aunt despatched her
to bring water from the well and scrub out the
dairy—clearly the heavier and less pleasant tasks were
to be reserved for her in future, and her dinner, when it
came, was meagre and unappetising. Hard work and
poor food she could bear if she had to, but her aunt's
tone towards her was harsher even than it had been
before, and it was quite clear that the servants had been
instructed not to speak to her. She had no one at all in
whom she could confide, no one even whom she could
ask about Nan.

The day seemed horribly long, with only her

thoughts for company, and by the end of it Deborah was exhausted and depressed. She cried herself to sleep that night, at the prospect of suffering endless days of this harsh loneliness.

The next day, as she had feared, began very much as yesterday. Once prayers and breakfast were over and the morning's water carried in, Deborah sat in a dim corner of the kitchen ineptly plucking and disembowelling a chicken. Since she had never actually performed the task herself before, and no one was willing to break her aunt's ruling and instruct her, it was a slow and messy business, and Deborah hated every minute of it. She had made very little progress by the time Betty found her.

'Mistress Foster wants you in the parlour,' she said in an undertone, as if even in carrying out her mistress's instructions she feared some retribution for speaking to the outcast.

Deborah laid aside the chicken, and gazed ruefully at her stained apron, and arms red and feathered to the elbow.

'Here, I'll give you a hand,' said Betty in a swift whisper, and led her to the well in the stable yard. The worst of the dirt was removed as quickly as possible, but there was no time for a change of clothing, and even with the apron removed Deborah's gown was far from clean.

'It will have to do,' said Deborah. 'Thank you.' She resisted a longing to stay behind and ask if Betty knew what had become of Nan. She could not risk her aunt's anger if she were long in answering her summons. As she hurried through the house she wondered apprehensively why she was wanted.

In the parlour with her aunt sat the quiet, kindly figure of Robert Fanshawe, the minister. Deborah had not seen him since that day when he had brought her home, and now the past came back to her in a rush. The delightful moments of escape, the magical castle, the minister's friendliness; and then her captivity, coming so soon afterwards, and all it meant. Now she dropped a respectful curtsy, and stood quietly with her hands folded in front of her, to hear what her aunt had to say.

'Deborah, Master Fanshawe here has been kind enough to come enquiring after your well-being. I have told him everything, including the position you hold in this house at present. He wishes to speak alone with you, and I hope you will give him your full attention. He has your salvation at heart as much as any of us.'

Deborah glanced at the minister, but his expression told her nothing. He looked simply grave and thoughtful, waiting for her aunt to leave them. Now, she supposed, she must prepare herself for another catalogue of her supposed sins. As the door closed behind Mistress Foster, she straightened her shoulders and faced her new accuser.

'I am glad that you escaped alive and unhurt from your ordeal,' Robert Fanshawe began mildly. The pleasantly conversational tone startled her; but she was still ready to leap at once on what he had—deliberately, she supposed—left unsaid.

'Has my aunt told you what she believes ... happened ... to me?' she asked, a little hesitantly. Though she had no doubt at all that he knew the whole story, as Susan Foster saw it.

'Yes,' he replied calmly. His grey eyes travelled over her, taking in the stained gown and the smear of chicken blood across the forehead which had escaped the hasty washing. 'Perhaps you would like to sit down and tell me exactly what happened.'

She was astonished: did he not, then, believe her aunt's story? Or did he simply hope to have her guilt confirmed from her own mouth? That, she decided, must be it. After all, it was always expected that the sinner should confess his sins before renouncing his evil past. But it was a relief at least to sit down on the stool which stood close to her, facing the minister across the room.

After that, she did not quite know where to begin. She gazed down for a little while at her clasped hands, and then raised her head to meet Master Fanshawe's eyes, quietly expectant—and even, though she hardly dared to believe it, gentle with compassion. 'What do you want me to say?' she asked.

'Whatever is true. All that you can remember from the time Nan left you in the coach.'

That distracted her from her story, and she broke in quickly, 'Have you seen Nan lately? Do you know where she is? My uncle dismissed her, and no one will tell me what's become of her.'

'She is in my sister's house, four miles from here. She is well, and if she gives good service she will be sure of a secure position. And if I see fit, I can take word of you to her. Will that satisfy you?'

'Oh yes,' said Deborah, with genuine relief and gratitude. 'I was so afraid she might have nowhere to go.'

'She was wise enough to come to me: that is how I first had word that you were home. So now I want to hear your story.'

'Yes,' Deborah said, and bent her head, frowning with the effort to remember, to tell her tale honestly and yet without betraying her secret. 'I was taken,' she began, 'through the woods, and then blindfolded, so I should not see where I went. It was damp and dark, like a dungeon, I suppose; but they gave me a bed and food, and I was not ill-used——'

'They?' he broke in. 'How many were there?'

'Two. The man they call Captain Black, and his servant.'

'The servant who is now dead, they say, and the man they've taken?'

'Yes.' She raised her head sharply. 'Master Fanshawe, that is almost all there is to tell. I came out' —she felt her colour rising—'as I went in. They did not touch me in—that way.' 'Not that way,' she thought, 'but the memory of his arms about me makes my body ache.'

The minister gazed at her for a long time, and she returned his gaze directly, unafraid. After a while he nodded.

'So you are a maid still. I am glad. But you must not judge your good aunt and uncle too harshly for finding it impossible to believe you. It is natural for them to think as they do, for you are young and beautiful and you have passed three or four days in the company of a notorious wrongdoer. Many people would have turned you from the house for that. I am sure you will be patient under this trouble, and accept it in the right spirit.'

'What right spirit?' thought Deborah, with an inward flash of anger. But she was silent, and only the brightness of her eyes showed him what she felt.

She wondered then, watching him, if he believed all he had said to her. Something in his expression seemed to suggest that he was almost as indignant at the injustice of her treatment as she was herself. After all, what could he do to help her, except perhaps try to persuade her uncle and aunt to treat her more kindly? But she knew that would be difficult even for a man so well-respected as the minister to do.

Perhaps he realised how helpless he was as he sat watching her now, for he was as silent as she, as if he could not think of anything consoling to say. It was a little comfort at least that he believed her, in spite of everything: she felt just a very little less lonely because of it. She had reached that conclusion when she remembered that there was something far more vital to her than her aunt's good opinion on which she needed his help.

'Master Fanshawe,' she began slowly, 'I am in need of advice——'

'Yes?' She knew that he sensed some other unsuspected sin, so far hidden, and she was annoyed to find that she blushed. 'It is something I don't want my uncle and aunt to know of,' she said quickly.

'Then you can be sure it will go no further without your agreement,' he reassured her.

'This man—this Captain Black——' she went on. 'He did not wrong me in any way, except in taking me prisoner. He . . . he did nothing to hurt me, or ill-use me. In fact,' she enlarged, her eyes raised candidly to his face, 'I think I can say he used me well, kindly, in his way. Because of that, I do not like to think that they will hang him because of me. Is there anything I can do to let them know that he is not the wicked man they think him?'

He shook his head wonderingly.

'It's a rare spirit of charity indeed that wants to save the life of a man who has brought you to this.' He indicated her dishevelled appearance. 'Or is it rather a rare kind of man?' He raised an eyebrow questioningly, and then said quickly: 'No, I don't expect an answer. Let's leave it at that. You asked me a question, and I'll reply as best I can. To be honest I don't know what you can do. I suppose it is possible that if there is little evidence against him beyond your own case, then if you were to appear in court and make a plea for his life on the grounds of his kindness towards you, it might move them to leniency. But I rather think there'll be other charges against him, besides yours. He's a notorious enough man, goodness knows. The chances are that they've more than enough to hang him without you. And I don't think it would help your good name to plead for him—nor, I think, would your uncle and aunt allow it.'

'If it would help him I would do it if it killed me,' Deborah declared fiercely.

'Yes,' said Robert Fanshawe wryly, 'I believe you would. And I have no right to encourage you in disobedience. But I will go to Maidstone and make some enquiries, to see if I can learn how strong the case is against him—a well-greased palm in the right place goes a long way—and then I'll let you know what I hear. Will that satisfy you?'

He had no need of an answer, looking at her face, glowing with relief and pleasure as it was.

'Oh, thank you!' she exclaimed. 'I think I can bear anything now, knowing that you are helping me.'

He thought then how very much she had changed from the girl he remembered. It was not just that she was tired and ill-used and dirty, but in spite of it there was a new confidence in her, a new defiant spirit. Before, she would have accepted all that had happened to her meekly, sadly, without complaint. Now the rebellion, the sense of justice, some depth of emotion which must always have been a part of her had burst forth with a new courage. Something had awakened her, and the timid girl had become all at once a woman with a mind and a determination of her own.

And one who was all the lovelier for the change, he added to himself; and then he went on to wonder again about the man who had taken her prisoner.

'I will take my leave of you now,' was all he said, still in that restrained but kindly tone. 'I make no promises and hold out no hope, but I'll do what I can. I'll call again as soon as I have news.'

Deborah watched him go, with a new warmth at her

heart. He had not told her that he felt for her plight or that he understood her feelings, or least of all that he would do everything in his power to act as her friend. But he had no need to say it. She had lost Nan, but nothing her aunt could do could take this friend from her, for was he not the one man against whom the door would never be closed? She returned to the kitchen and the remains of the chicken, feeling as if she could face the most dreadful of tasks with cheerfulness.

But it was not always so easy, even now. It was hard to be cheerful, to remember that she was not entirely alone, when day after day passed in a long succession of unpleasant, wearying, dirty tasks, to be performed alone and in silence with only her aunt's criticism and her uncle's preaching to relieve the monotony. Even the food—still eaten in her room—was plainer and less plentiful than before. She was never allowed away from the house; she did not even go as far as the garden, for her work restricted her to the area of the kitchens and the stable yard, and even that little breath of fresh air was only permitted briefly, at rare intervals, when the job she had to do gave her no choice.

She welcomed the mealtimes, and the moment when she went exhausted to bed at the end of a long day, because then she was at last alone, but not lonely. She had her thoughts and her memories, and however painful they might be at times, it was better than the loneliness of incessant work amongst people who were not allowed to speak to her.

She sensed, sometimes, that they pitied her. A look or a gesture when her aunt was out of sight showed what they felt; but it was little enough comfort in long hours of silence. She began to wonder if she might be better off if she were to run away; but she had enough common sense to know that it was foolish to think of it. For as yet she had no control over her fortune, and without it, penniless in a world which she had found unvaryingly hostile, she would be helpless.

Unless of course she could find a friend to help her. That she put on one side, as a future possibility. Meanwhile, she could do nothing until she knew what she must do to help the man she loved.

It was five days after Robert Fanshawe's visit that Sir Edward Biddulph came to the house. Deborah saw him as she hurried to the kitchen after dinner, coming in out of the rain in answer to her aunt's welcoming greeting. She did not wait to discover if she had been seen, but went on her way as quickly as possible. She owed Sir Edward no loyalty now, and could avoid him with an entirely clear conscience. That was one compensation brought by her new status.

If it had not been raining so hard, Deborah would not have been chosen for the usually relatively pleasant task of going to the herb garden for some parsley. As it was, none of the other servants was eager to brave the drenching torrent and the cook, mindful of Mistress Foster's instructions, sought out Deborah in the cool dryness of the dairy, and ordered her out into the rain.

She did not mind. It seemed a very long time since she had left the smells of kitchen and stables behind her and enjoyed the sweetness of the garden, late roses and grass and sodden herbs. And the cold freshness of the rain was exhilarating and cleansing. She walked slowly, lifting her face to the sky, letting the water soak her to the skin, savouring every moment of freedom alone in the fragrant garden. The dirt and humiliation alike of the past days seemed to fall away from her.

She gathered the parsley piece by piece, making every moment last as long as she could; and then she made her way on through the herb garden and under the clipped yew archway into the orderly rose garden.

There, at the far end, was a small arbour, partly hidden
from sight by a hanging curtain of entwining rose and
ivy. She sat down on the stone seat there and closed her
eyes, and felt the peace of the garden soak into her as
thoroughly as had the rain. She was so much at her ease
that she did not hear the footsteps on the path, and did
not know anyone was there until the man lifted aside
the creeper and bent his head to come in beside her.

'Sir Edward!' She sprang to her feet in dismay, and
he reached out a hand to urge her back on to the seat.

'Stay a while, Deborah,' he said. 'I should enjoy your
company for a little time.' He sat crossways on the seat
beside her, his knees barring her escape. She retreated
as far as she could into the corner of the arbour: even in
the dimness here she could see an unfamiliar glint in his
eyes which she did not like.

'My aunt said that you had ended our betrothal,' she
said stiffly.

'Of course. I had no choice. But'—he laid a hand on
her knee—'that need not mean the end of everything
between us.' He broke off, leaving her to draw her own
conclusions. She was afraid that she knew what he
meant, but hoped she was wrong.

'It can only mean that,' she said with great emphasis,
and tried to push his hand away.

'Ah, but that is because you believe you have no
choice but to accept your uncle's will for you. While you
are living as his servant that must be so. But there is
another possibility open to you, a way of escape.'

He caught her interest then, and she looked up
sharply, the intruding hand forgotten.

'What way? What can I do?'

He lifted a finger, and shook it at her.

'Ah, now you want to hear me! Listen then, my little
cousin, and I will tell you exactly what you can do to
come from slavery to comfort and happiness in a few

short hours. I do not say that your uncle and aunt have been unduly harsh, or unjust; but perhaps they need not have gone to these lengths to bring you to a sense of your sin. That is as may be. I offer you comfort and protection, an untroubled life of simple pleasure.'

Deborah's eyes widened.

'I do not see how you can give me any of these things.'

He smiled and touched her cheek, and she tried not to show how she disliked the touch, for after all he was trying to help her.

'Then I will tell you, my moppet. There is a wing of the house at Sandwell which is never used. There you could have your own chamber, a little parlour, a little haven all of your own. You would have your own maid to wait upon you and bear you company, and at times the freedom of the garden for your leisure. Whatever whim or fancy you had, for food or clothes or jewellery, would be yours. What do you say to that?'

She tried to imagine herself at the centre of the idly luxurious life he painted for her, and failed; but her astonishment was clear for him to see. She said at last:

'But what of your mother? And my aunt and uncle? What would they say? They would not think it right that I should be happy.'

'I am master in my own house,' said Sir Edward with dignity. 'You need have no dealings with my mother. As for your aunt and uncle, they will accept it as for the best, and be willing to come to some arrangement, as your guardians, so that you may have the use of your inheritance for your own comfort. I know there will be no difficulty there. Come now, what do you say? Will you come to my little haven, and live there without a care in the world?'

It sounded too good to be true, the comfortable rooms, the garden, best of all the relief of being alone, with Nan for company, if she could choose her own servant, and no one to trouble her. She did not like Sir Edward, but she was moved by the generosity of what he offered. Or was he in fact so generous? Was there some condition he had failed to mention? Something she could not accept?

'Why are you doing this for me? What can I mean to you now, if you do not think me fit to be your wife? Surely you cannot think me fit either to be used so kindly?'

'Not at all,' he said, bending closer to her. 'You can no longer live among us as a woman worthy of respect and honour, but you can live secluded, with all the comforts you could wish, under my protection. Discreetly, of course, which is why you would not have all the freedom you might wish for. And my visits to you must not be made too openly. But I do not foresee any problem.' His hand moved now from her knee and rested, clammily caressing, on her throat. His breath, hot and unpleasant, reached her, uncomfortably close. His voice was hoarse and thickened with emotion.

'I can think only of the joy to have you there, the delights of hours passed in your company—the long nights—oh, Deborah, say you will come——'

It was then that she understood him completely. How stupid, how unutterably naïve she had been not to have known at once what he meant! His hands were pushing the coif from her hair, his mouth bending close to hers, his heavy body lurching against her, defiling the path which another man had already taken, oh so differently! She felt sick, and then furiously angry. She turned her head, and bit sharply at the caressing hand, and then seized his moment of pain and astonishment to push her way past him and away along the path back to the house.

Mercifully she remembered as she passed the herb garden that she had left the parsley behind in her flight, and paused just long enough to gather some more; for the cook—and her aunt, who was now waiting for her in the kitchen—were angry enough at her long absence without that extra reason for their wrath. They threatened her with a whipping, and she knew that next time it would be more than a threat.

But for all that, as she returned wet and shivering and ignored to the dairy, she knew that there was, after all, something a good deal worse than this present bleak existence. Whatever they thought of her, however much they ill-used her, at least she was at peace with herself. Knowing what, in a weak moment, she might perhaps have become, she was even a little thankful for what she had.

CHAPTER
NINE

DEBORAH did not expect to hear any more of her confrontation with Sir Edward in the garden: no one, she was sure, had seen them together, and he himself would surely be unlikely to mention so discreditable and humiliating an incident. She was consequently caught completely off her guard when her aunt sought her out as she scrubbed the stone flags of the kitchen floor at the end of the day's cooking, and took her to one side in the empty brew-house, where they were not likely to be disturbed. One glance at Susan Foster's face told Deborah she was extremely displeased; but then when was she ever anything else, these days?

'Sir Edward tells me,' she began without preliminary, 'that you used him most discourteously when he spoke with you in the garden this morning.'

Deborah's head lifted swiftly from its meek pose, her breath indrawn with astonishment.

'What did he say?' she asked with genuine curiosity.

'Are you denying that you behaved towards him with none of the respect due to a gentleman of rank from a girl fallen as low as you are now?'

'Yes,' said Deborah quickly and with anger, 'I am denying it. He insulted me—how, I won't say, because it makes no difference—but it would have been an insult to any woman.'

'May I remind you that you are now too low for insult? Don't give yourself airs. It does not make your position any better.'

At that, all Deborah's resentment rose in her, and she

could contain herself no longer.

'How can you go on telling me how low I have fallen, when I have given you my word that it is not true? Does my word count for nothing against your opinion? Because I am young and friendless you think you can use me just as you please, and no one will think you do wrong. Well, I think it—you and my uncle are unjust and cruel and stupid, too sure of your own righteousness to think anyone else is worthy of trust and respect. You told me you were doing your Christian duty in treating me as you have—if that is Christianity then I think I would rather be a heathen and know nothing of it!'

She knew long before she ended that she had gone too far: she watched the colour rise and deepen in her aunt's face as she spoke, saw the knuckles close and whiten, the eyes darken with anger. But she had to go on, just this once, and let her aunt know what she felt. When she fell silent at last Mistress Foster said nothing for several moments, but stood breathing fast, trying to control her anger enough to speak. At last she said:

'Have you finished? Good. Because I shall not stand here idly to listen to the wicked abuse of a depraved and ungrateful girl. You have only convinced me the more that we have not simply been just, but generous in our treatment of you. Go to your room at once, and wait there.'

This time Deborah knew she could not escape the whipping, and she did not. Later, weary and sore from the expression of her aunt's anger upon her, she lay alone in the dark on her bed and considered the day's events. Perhaps if she had been prepared for her aunt's accusation this evening she would not have given voice to her anger so openly; and she was still astonished, thinking back, that Sir Edward had spoken of the incident at all. Certainly he would not have told them

exactly what passed, but surely he must have feared
that Deborah might tell the truth if she were asked? Did
he assume that they would not believe her? Or, worse,
did he think that they would not care very much?

'They will accept it as for the best ... be willing to
come to some arrangement ... there will be no difficulty
there,' so he had said of her aunt and uncle when laying
the proposition before her. Almost as if he had known
that they would connive at his seduction of their niece,
find it a convenient solution for her to become his
mistress.

But that was preposterous: the Fosters were respectable, godly people, and even if the upright Sir Edward
had been led astray by his passions, they had no such
excuse. They could not, surely, wish such a fate on her
when they had shown such violent outrage at the mer-
est suspicion of it at the hands of another man?

On the other hand, said that chilling little voice in
her head, which had not fully left her in peace since the
moment in her captivity when doubt of her uncle's
motives had first reared its ugly head; on the other
hand, a woman who had fallen so far as to become little
better than a whore, heiress or not, would be unlikely to
be sought in marriage by anyone. There would be no
legitimate children, no one to question that the inheritance should go anywhere but to the nearest kinsfolk, the
devoted uncle and aunt so concerned for her moral
welfare.

No, no! Deborah thrust her hands over her ears as if
there were indeed someone standing at her side to
whisper these dreadful suggestions to her. In any case,
she told herself firmly, they had told her only too plainly
that she had already fallen too low for a respectable
marriage. If she were Sir Edward's mistress it would
make no difference in the eyes of the world. It was
ridiculous to think they could be planning her downfall

so deviously, so coolly, with such deliberate calculation.

She thrust the thought resolutely aside, and set herself to think of the man she loved, the one glimmer of light in her life, and to send up a little prayer that the light would not totally be extinguished, if there was any way out.

In the morning she was summoned again to the parlour, where the minister waited as before to speak with her. This time she was not apprehensive but went in eagerly, sat down—cautiously, for she was sore still—and waited for him to give her his news.

'Did you find out anything?' she asked when he did not speak at once. He smiled gently at her impatience, and then as quickly subsided into gravity.

'I am afraid there is not much comfort in it for you,' he told her, his expression rueful.

The eagerness faded, and a great weight seemed to fall on her, crushing out the small, carefully harboured flicker of hope.

'Is there nothing I can do then?'

'I'm afraid it does not look as though there is,' he admitted. 'I went into it all very thoroughly for you in Maidstone, asking questions wherever I could, discreetly of course, and I learnt a great deal. Most of it not in your Captain's favour.'

He glanced at her, concerned at the bleakness of her eyes. 'Deborah, I am sorry; but it seems there are other charges, serious ones, quite enough to hang a man without need of your case at all. Highway robbery, theft, even a doubtful murder, which was probably a simple accident but does not look good set beside the others. Any one of these would be enough to hang him, I think. But the most serious charge, which may not be brought against him for lack of evidence, is still likely to weigh most heavily in his disfavour. There is some talk that he was a Royalist spy, plotting the downfall of the Republic——'

So they knew, or at least suspected. She could think of nothing to say, faced with news so hopeless. She had not realised until now how much she had expected that Robert Fanshawe would find some solution for her, some way she could help and make everything come right. And instead there was this.

'I think they have no real evidence of the last charge, which may mean it's all a rumour, for the government's intelligence system has always been good. If there was any truth in it, any concrete evidence, they would know of it. But the suspicion may be enough to make his conviction certain on the other charges. A highwayman is bad enough, a Royalist highwayman unendurable.' He made a helpless gesture with his hands. 'I'm sorry. There's not much cheer in that for you, I'm afraid.'

'No,' she agreed sadly. 'Do you not think I should go to the court and plead for him even so? Just in the hope that it might work?'

He shook his head.

'I think they would only see that as further proof of his perfidy. They would think as your aunt and uncle do, and assume he had seduced you for his own ends——'

'But they all think that anyway, don't they? I could tell them it wasn't true. If they all believe that's what he did, it might move them.'

'I don't suppose they do all believe that,' said the minister unguardedly, and then paused, realising what he had implied. Deborah, too, saw the implication at once.

'Then my aunt was wrong when she said the world would think me a fallen woman——' she said slowly, half questioning.

'I'm sure *she* believes it to be true,' broke in Robert. His tone was too hasty to be entirely convincing, and she gazed at him with wide candid eyes for a few moments, until he began to feel uncomfortable.

'Tell me,' she said at last, 'do you think that if my uncle and aunt had welcomed me home, and continued to use me as they had before, as kindly as they know how,' which isn't much, said her tone, 'do you think then that no one at all would have thought I had done anything wrong?'

'Not no one at all,' Robert said with obvious reluctance. 'There are always some who will think the worst, but most would have only pity for your plight.'

She knew that he had found that moment of honesty very difficult, but she was grateful for it, and accepted his need to go on quickly.

'But you mustn't hold that against your elders, Deborah.' He had, like everyone else, she noticed, dropped the respectful 'Mistress Halsey'; but from him the simple 'Deborah' sounded only kind, and affectionate. 'They believe that they have only your welfare at heart. Perhaps they misjudged things a little, but then who does not, some time or another? They will do you no lasting harm, as long as you do not allow yourself to become bitter or resentful.'

'It would have been lasting harm, if Sir Edward had his way,' Deborah returned without thinking, and then wished she had not spoken so hastily. The words had slipped out in an unguarded moment.

'What do you mean?' asked her companion. She blushed deeply.

'Nothing,' she said, 'it was nothing.'

But he pressed her for an answer and she told him, reluctantly and briefly, what had happened in the garden yesterday. She had not imagined that the quiet-mannered minister could look so angry, his grey eyes alight under sharply frowning brows.

'That is unpardonable!' he exclaimed. 'How dared he so insult you! I've half a mind to speak to him of it——' She broke in with a horrified protest, and he relaxed a little. 'Very well, then, I won't. But did you tell your aunt? I hope so.'

Deborah told him what had passed with her aunt, and this time his reaction was quite different. She sensed the anger smouldering at white heat, but he was silent, his mouth set in a grim line.

'Deborah,' he asked at last, 'how long is it before you have control over your inheritance? How long are you to be your uncle's ward?'

'I don't know,' she admitted, wondering why he should ask.

'Then I'll try and find out. I think perhaps you ought to set up your own establishment somewhere as soon as you can, with good reliable servants, of course, in a respectable neighbourhood. But we'd better not talk of that now. It's for the future. Try and be patient: one day things will be easier, I'm sure.'

Then he too, she thought, believes that my uncle and aunt have set out to blacken my name, even perhaps to lead me into something worse. He will not admit it, but he knows that they treated me so unkindly on my return because then everyone would believe I had fallen, and I would be cast out; a woman no one would stoop to marry. And if Sir Edward had made me his mistress it would have made doubly sure, just in case there were still those who believed me innocent.

She shivered. Perhaps—small crumb of comfort that it was—they had not planned this deliberately; perhaps everything had conveniently fallen into place to suit their hopes. Perhaps they really believed they were acting for the best. But she knew she would never convince herself that their motives were without malice: too much told against them, too much which suggested that they had hoped Captain Black would do their work for them, and when she returned alive they had found this subtler means ready to hand, and used it discreetly but without mercy. For the first time since returning to Pembridge Deborah was really afraid.

She knew Robert sensed her fear, for he reached out and took her hand.

'If ever you need a friend, send for me. I shall come often to see you. No one will ever refuse entrance to me in this house, so you know I can help you to the best of my powers. Now I think I must go. Keep up your courage.'

She held him back for a moment. 'Will they call me to give evidence at the trial?'

'No,' he said, pausing in the doorway, 'I think not. Your uncle has let them know that you have been shamed enough without appearing as a public witness—and I'm afraid they do not need your evidence.'

His last sight was of her stricken face, white, rigid with the effort needed to control the tears; and then he left her, angry, distressed, but most of all deeply disturbed. He would not leave it so long before he came again.

So it was that one grey damp day in November it was Robert Fanshawe who brought word to Pembridge Hall that Captain Black had been brought to trial, found guilty, and condemned to death.

There were two days left. It was Saturday when Robert Fanshawe brought them the news, and the Captain was to hang on Monday, at daybreak.

The full horror of it sank only slowly into Deborah's brain, and then lingered, hammering its message into her consciousness, that grim phrase 'to hang on Monday', 'to hang on Monday'. The colour drained from her face, leaving it ashen, her eyes wide pools of darkness in the surrounding pallor, and she swayed dizzily. Her aunt, unavoidably present, was watching her with marked interest, a question clearly close to her lips. Robert Fanshawe moved unobtrusively to Deborah's side, and slid a supporting hand beneath her elbow.

'I think this has brought it all back to her,' he said quickly. 'She went through a great deal, and it takes a long time for the healing to be complete. It does no good for her to be reminded of what happened.'

Mercifully, Susan Foster seemed to accept the hastily invented explanation, and her attention moved on to other matters. Deborah was despatched to the kitchen while her elders talked, and moved about aimlessly with no idea at all what she was doing until the minister came in from the stables to seek her out. He glanced round first to be sure that they were not overheard.

'I am going now,' he said gently, 'but I had to see you first. I am sorry to be the bearer of such news. I think I know your feelings, but I'm afraid it was only as we expected. You could have done nothing: I was there, and heard the case against him. It was quite clear that the verdict was never in doubt.'

Deborah had raised her head swiftly at his admission that he had been at the trial; when he had finished she asked in a low voice:

'Did you see him? How was he?'

'I saw him,' Robert answered, his eyes on her face. 'I think I understand you a little better for it. He was proud and unafraid—by the end of the trial the crowd in the court was eating out of his hand. You need have no fear for his courage.'

'I know that,' she said, bending her head again to hide the tears. 'I wish—oh, I wish—there was something I could do. Perhaps I should have gone to the trial somehow, and spoken up. Perhaps I would have been sure then that I could do no more.'

'Believe me,' the minister said earnestly, 'it would only have made matters worse. I am quite sure of that.'

'But they could not be worse,' she half-sobbed in reply.

'At least he will have some sympathy, perhaps, from the crowd. If they thought him a seducer of young girls as well as all the rest they would have jeered him all the way to the gallows—Be brave, Deborah. If it helps, remember that he is not afraid. And if this is the worst moment for you, it can only get better. I know you have courage: use it now, when you need it most.'

She tried to thank him for his sympathy, but no words came: he clasped her hand for a moment, and then he took his leave of her.

The day passed in a dark haze of anguish, of which she remembered nothing except that it was unbearably long. But the time did come at last when she was alone in her room, and could sit in the dark on the window seat and gaze out into the lesser blackness of the night. It was cold, but she was too miserable to notice. The moment when she had been held in the arms of the man she loved seemed now like a dream, a golden memory long past. But to know that there would never even be the remotest hope of the dream's return was more than she could bear.

She had seen a hanging once in London—her father had thought it a necessary part of a child's education to be warned of the penalty for wrongdoing—and she remembered it now: only in place of the ghastly face of the hanged man was the face of the man she loved. She could not think, she could not pray, she had only that terrible waking nightmare in her head and the tearing longing inside her which cried out for one last living sight of him, perhaps even one final moment in his arms. Something more to take with her into the darkness of the future than that silent unsatisfactory parting at the crossroads.

It would not matter, she was sure, if it made him angry to see her once more, if in facing him she were to learn only that he was utterly indifferent to her. She would have seen him again, looked on him with a love she acknowledged, imprinted every line of his beloved form on her memory to treasure in the empty years to come.

The longing in her crystallised slowly, irrevocably, into a decision: she must see him again. She would brave any punishment on earth to have that last meeting with him. She knew she would have to do it all alone: she could not ask the minister to aid her in deceiving her guardians, and if she did not deceive them then she had no hope of seeing him. Robert Fanshawe was her friend, but she knew he could not, in his position, encourage her in disobedience.

She set herself as calmly as she could to plan her escape. There would be little enough opportunity, she knew: she was never allowed further than the stable yard except on that one best-forgotten occasion, and then rarely alone. There were also fellow servants, grooms and others, about in the stables, so that she had no hope of borrowing a horse unobserved to take her to Maidstone: in any case, she was a very inexperienced rider. No, she decided, she could not leave in daylight, for almost certainly she would be seen.

Yet at night she would too easily lose her way, and then come too late to see him. She decided at last that the escape must be made in darkness, and she must then hide somewhere close by until daylight, when she could find her way more easily. And it must be tonight, for there was so little time left, and about fifteen miles between Pembridge and the man she loved.

First, to leave the house. If she tried to leave by the

door she knew she would be discovered. Her uncle's
two great hounds kept watch in the hall, and there was
no other way but that to reach the outside. It was not far
from her window to the garden, and with more than her
usual courage, for she did not like heights at all, she
might do it: she had no choice but to do it.

'Now,' she thought, 'I need stout shoes and a good
warm cloak; and money.'

Gaolers, she knew, had to be bribed if one wanted
their help, and there might be other calls for money on
her way. She had not carried money on her person since
she came to Pembridge, for when had she had need to
spend it? But on her journey here from London she
knew she had carried a substantial sum—about four or
five guineas, she thought—with her in the coach. Just
possibly it might still be in her room.

It was. In a small leather drawstring purse beneath
the heavy grey folds of her winter cloak, stored away in
the chest at the foot of the bed. She pushed the purse
into the pocket of her gown, and took out the cloak: it
was long, with a wide concealing hood, ideal for her
purpose. She put on her sturdiest shoes, her most un-
becoming coif, and then drew the cloak about her. Next
she took the sheets from the bed and knotted them
together into a makeshift but serviceable rope. Tied to
the bedpost, they did not quite reach the ground outside the window, but there would not be far to jump at
the end: mercifully only the parlour lay below her room,
deserted even by dogs at this time of night.

Shoes; money; cloak: she was ready. She crept to the
window, too anxious to reach the Captain to be afraid of
what she was about to do, and edged her way over the
sill and down until she hung just outside, her feet
resting on the lintel of the parlour window below. Then
one last swing on the sheets and she reached the end of
them, and fell the last few feet to the ground.

She wished she knew some way of returning the sheets to her room, so they would not know at once what she had done, but there was nothing she could do about it. She scrambled to her feet, pulled her cloak about her, and ran softly across the garden towards the blackness of the surrounding wall. Something she had done must have disturbed the dogs, for she heard the first round of frantic barking as she ran as fast as she could away from the house.

She reached the lane beyond the garden in safety, and then stood gathering her breath, wondering where to go now. The woods? Along the lane? She wished she knew where they were most likely to search for her first. What if they were to send the dogs after her?

She remembered hearing that dogs could not follow a trail across water, and that there was a stream a little further on forming the boundary between her uncle's land, and his neighbours. It crossed the lane and disappeared into the woods. She turned left and ran until the hazy moonlight marked the silver line crossing the track, and then selected what she felt to be the deepest part of the stream and splashed her way through it.

So much (she hoped) for the dogs: now for a hiding-place. An outbuilding or barn of some kind would seem the wisest choice, warm and sheltering, with something stored in it which might serve to conceal her. A little further still a track led to the next farmhouse, and passed a narrow hay barn: she found her way there without difficulty, pushed open the door, and crept inside. The hay was stacked almost to the roof. She looked quickly for the best place to hide before closing the door and shutting out the dim light, and then crept in the darkness to the farthest corner, made a hollow in the fragrant softness, and lay down to rest.

She did not expect to sleep, though once or twice she dozed briefly, but it was tormenting to lie here without

moving when there was so far still to go. If only she had
known her way about better; but she had never had any
opportunity to learn. The hours passed slowly, painfully slowly. By the time the first dawn greyness slunk
round the barn doors she was stiff and cold and very
thankful that it was time to be moving.

It was a bitter morning, the mist dense above the
frosty ground, and she could see little more than she
had at night time. She was grateful for the warmth of
the heavy cloak, and pulled it closer about her. She
walked quickly in what she hoped was the right direction, trying to bring some warmth into her limbs by the
swiftness of the movement. The sound of her shoes
seemed to echo in the cold silence of the early morning,
so that she was sure her pursuers would find her in no
time at all—if they were indeed in pursuit.

She hoped that her guardians would have assumed
that she had started on her way at once, to get as far as
possible by daybreak; and surely they would not guess
where she was making for. She could trust Robert
Fanshawe not to betray her even if he suspected her
destination. But if they had gone out last night in search
of her they might meet her on the road as they returned
empty-handed to Pembridge. That possibility had not
occurred to her last night, and it frightened her now,
giving greater speed to her pace, and causing her to
glance anxiously behind her from time to time as she
went.

As it happened she met no one, except an old woman
gathering sticks near her cottage, and a woodcutter on
his way to work. On each occasion she pulled the hood
lower about her face and bent her head, and she
thought she was scarcely noticed. When she came to a
farm or village she walked more quickly, or sought a
side-lane to take her past unobserved.

After a while, as she began to feel warmer and no sign

nor sound was there of any pursuit, another anxiety began to trouble her. She was hungry. In her unhappiness the day before she had eaten no dinner, which meant that her last meal had been yesterday's breakfast. It seemed an age ago now, and she wondered what she would do for food if the need became desperate. Apart from that the walk would almost have been enjoyable, had there not been so tormenting a reason for it. She could not remember when she had last walked for long in the open air—on that day before her capture, she supposed—and it was a pleasure at least to experience the fresh air and exercise.

She came to a village at last where a throng of people moving in one direction down the main street reminded her forcibly that it was Sunday. She hesitated for a moment, wondering what she should do, and then attached herself quietly to a large family group and followed them, one among their accompanying servants, until they came to the church. Then she slipped out of sight behind the building and waited there until all were inside and the vigorous strains of a psalm reached her on the air. She was not so conspicuous now, a lone traveller walking quickly away from the village.

So it went on. Dogs barked at her sometimes, or a passer-by caused her a moment's anxiety. But by now at least most people were in church, and those who weren't were not inclined to question the actions of the hunched, sober figure of indeterminate sex and age who passed them. Twice she was reassured by signposts directing the traveller to Maidstone: she was on the right road, if nothing else.

The hunger grew worse, and Deborah began to feel very weary, her steps growing slower and slower, until she longed to rest. But it must already be nearly midday, and the days were short at this time of year. And by dawn tomorrow it would be too late. Would they let her into the prison after dark? she wondered. And then she prayed, 'Don't let me be too late, please don't let me be too late!'

But even that fear could not add to her failing strength.

She was roused from her despairing exhaustion by the sound of a wheeled horse-drawn vehicle approaching quickly behind her. She glanced sharply round: it was a wagon, something like a carrier's cart, driven by a cheerful-looking burly red-faced man. Even though she had never seen him before, she stepped back quickly into the shelter of the trees for fear he should recognise her.

But he had seen her, and called out: 'Going far, mistress? Care for a ride?'

Deborah looked up in silence, wondering whether she dared trust him. She was so tired, and so desperate to be there in time, and he did not look as if he meant her harm.

On the other hand she believed it was against the law for him to be travelling on a Sunday—it was certainly a sin—and perhaps that made him untrustworthy. Perhaps, on the contrary, it made him less likely to betray her. The weariness won.

'Maidstone,' she said faintly.

''Op up then,' he advised her, and reached down to help her on to the seat beside him. 'Not a good day to be walking,' he added, and produced a tattered blanket from somewhere behind him. ''Ere, put that over you. Keep out the cold a bit, like.'

'Thank you,' she said, thankful for the meagre comfort.

He clicked his tongue to the sturdy if unbeautiful bay horse which pulled the wagon, and the vehicle's jolting unstable progress along the road was resumed.

'I'll not ask why you're journeying on the Sabbath,

when all good folks should be at their pious exercising,'
he went on with a wink. 'As one sinner to another I
know when a question's out of order. Fancy a bite to eat
then?'

'Oh!—Yes!' she said eagerly, her last traces of suspicion evaporating. Surely this was her good angel?

'Take a look behind us there. You'll find a pasty—a
fine one, too, baked by my good woman last
night—we'll share it. There's an apple tart as well, or
so she said.'

Deborah found the food, and it was indeed delicious.
She felt restored and hopeful, her hunger gone, her
body rested, the wagon taking her at what seemed an
amazing speed on her way to Maidstone.

He had not tricked her in that either, for the mile
posts showed clearly how far there was to go, how much
nearer they were coming. Her companion was talka-
tive, but not intrusively so. He seemed to be glad of her
company, but did not mind that she said very little. The
shadow waited still at the end of the journey, but the
weight of her fear that she might not be in time had
gone.

Even so there was only about an hour of daylight left
by the time they reached the town. Thank goodness she
had met with her new friend, or she might have come
here to find it had all been in vain.

'Where do you want to be then, mistress?' the man
asked. She hesitated for a moment, and then said
boldly:

'The gaol, if you please.'

He shot a sideways look at her, full of understanding,
and her gratitude was the greater that he made no
comment, simply drove to the grim door and left her
there with a brief and gentle farewell, and a refusal of
any payment for his kindness.

'All the best, mistress!' was his parting call, and then

he was gone.

It took her some time to be admitted to the prison, at first because no one answered her hammering, and then because the money she held out was clearly insufficient. She was troubled at how much it had taken to gain entrance so far, for even now she had only bought herself the first step inside. The darkness and the stench were dreadful even here.

'I wish to see Captain Black,' she said to the round, unshaven gaoler who faced her.

'Do you now?' he said, leering at her, with a glimpse of broken and blackened teeth. 'Good thing it's not this time tomorrow. He'd be precious little company for you by then.'

She felt sick, and shrank back a little, pulling the cloak closer about her as if she were cold.

'It'll take a sweetener or two to see him, that I do know,' the man went on.

'How much?' she asked with fast-beating heart.

In the end it was all she had, but at least that was enough. He led her, keys jangling, along a dark passage dripping with moisture, loud with the noise of the over-crowded common gaol.

'The best chamber, he's got,' he said. 'All home comforts for the last night.' He spat on the ground before them. 'Make a good 'anging, I reckon. They like a fine gentleman out there.' He jerked with his thumb to indicate the outside world where the gallows waited, ready for its victim.

Deborah was shivering by the time the heavy studded door, with its metal grille, was reached. The gaoler peered in to reassure himself it was the right cell, and then turned the key and threw open the door.

'Visitor for you, Cap'n. 'Alf an hour, and no more.'

He turned to signal to Deborah to pass him into the cell. And it was then, faced with the moment she had longed for, that her courage failed her and she hesitated. What would he say, this condemned man faced with the girl who, however unwillingly, had brought him here? Would he know that she came in love, or would he think she came simply to gloat at his fall? Would he gaze at her harshly, coldly, or would she see for a moment a glimpse of the enigmatic something which might have been a warmer feeling?

'You going in or not?' demanded the gaoler, and she glanced up at him, drew a deep breath, and passed through the door. It banged shut behind her, the key turned, and she was alone with the prisoner.

CHAPTER
TEN

It was dark in there, that was the first thing Deborah noticed about it. A tiny high opening—scarcely big enough to be called a window—let in a faint light. She thought of her prison, but this was smaller, and higher, and smelt far worse: the stink of long usage, of hunger and degradation and imminent death.

And then she saw him, moving slowly to his feet from the low bench facing the door, his hair pale in the darkness; amazement, disbelief, visible on his face even in the dark.

'Mistress Halsey?' he asked uncertainly, his voice hoarse with emotion. 'What ... what are you doing here? Why have you come...?'

She longed to run across the little space between them, to throw her arms about him, to cry that love alone had brought her; but she could not. She stood gazing at him, silent, lost for words.

Her eyes had grown used to the darkness now, and she could see him better. He looked thinner, weary and wasted. But his eyes were clear, though there was uncertainty in them, suspicion even. Robert had been right: he was unafraid even now, when death faced him so nearly. Looking at him she felt overwhelmed with pity and grief, but most of all with her love for him. Now she was doubly sure of what she had always known: no one, ever, would hold her heart so completely as he did at this moment.

And yet, stupidly, with the minutes ticking relentlessly away she could think of nothing to say. Not because there was nothing, but because there was so much that a lifetime would not be long enough. A lifetime: her heart lurched as she remembered how very short his own lifetime was to be. She forced the stupid, commonplace words to the surface.

'I came ... to see you ... I wanted to ...'

He moved a little nearer, as if the better to see her face.

'Why?' he asked wryly. 'To enjoy the prospect of my death?'

She cried out sharply.

'No, oh no, not that! Never think that!'

He smiled then, so gently and so sweetly that she felt her bones melt to nothing and the tears filled her eyes.

'For that then I thank you,' he said, and took her hands for a moment in his cold fingers. 'It is kind of you, after all you suffered at my hands, to visit me like this.'

She shook her head, longing to say that it was not kindness which brought her but something more. Only she was too close to weeping to dare to speak.

He released her, and stood looking down at her, smiling still.

'In coming you have given me the opportunity I need to make my peace with you. I have not forgotten how angry you were that last night at the way I had used you. God knows I've had time enough to think of it still, and to realise how right you were. No danger which I faced, no hardship, not even the needs of the cause I served, could justify all I did to you. I can only ask your forgiveness, so that I may go to my death at peace with the world.'

She gazed back at him in an agony of grief and loss. So that was his pleasure in seeing her, to gain her forgiveness. She almost felt his anger would have been preferable. Her love meant nothing to him, for he did not even suspect that it was there, showed no sign at all of wanting it. She had thought it would be enough simply to see him, but she knew now how much she longed to hear that her love was returned. And that she would never hear, for it was the last thing on his mind, and had no part in his feeling for her. She swallowed, and accepted the bitter realisation, and gave him instead what he asked.

'I forgive everything,' she said in a low difficult voice. 'With all my heart.'

He took her hands again, and her heart leapt.

'I thank you for that,' he returned softly, and bent then to touch her forehead with his lips. A kiss, but so light, so brief, so without passion or emotion that it barely merited the name. It was no more than a gentle emphasis to his thanks, and a farewell.

She snatched her hands from his and turned sharply away, and the sobs tore at her, wild, uncontrollable.

'Mistress Halsey!' he cried, concerned, his touch gentle on her shoulder. 'Don't weep—for God's sake, if that's what it is, don't weep for me! I am not worthy of your tears.'

'I can't bear it! I can't bear to live without you!'

'Nonsense,' he said with a brisk cheerfulness which wrung her heart by its very lack of emotion. 'You will manage very well. Stop that now.'

She gulped down her tears and raised her eyes miserably to his. 'I wish there was some hope, even the least thread of hope, that you would be safe,' she said.

He smiled.

'You have given me a moment of the outside world by coming here today. As if you had spirited me away from this place for a little time. It's all I need.'

The words reached her slowly, making little sense, and then rearranged themselves, took shape, a new shape; and suddenly had a clear and imperative meaning. She drew back, her head raised, her eyes bright and eager, the despairing grief gone without trace.

'But that's it. Why did I not think of it before—is there still time? Here, take my cloak——'

He gazed at her in bewilderment.

'What are you talking about? Mistress Halsey, have you lost your senses?'

This time she managed a smile, faint but real.

'No, I think I have come to them instead. It is simple. I can't think why it took me so long. Here, you put on my clothes and leave here in my cloak. I am sure the gaoler scarcely saw my face in that hood. He would not know the difference. You'd have to stoop a little, but no one will notice in the dark—Come now, quickly, take this——'

He ignored the proffered cloak, and laughed in astonishment.

'Mistress Halsey, you amaze me! Your generosity takes my breath away. But it's not very practical, is it? Just think for a minute, what——'

'Of course it's practical,' she broke in impatiently. 'Only if you waste time arguing the gaoler will be back and it will be too late.'

He grasped her by the shoulders, still smiling.

'Think about it, mistress. What of you? He will not think he's seeing me sitting there still, if he sees your little figure shivering there in your shift. Or do you intend that I should smuggle you out with me under the cloak? It may be large, but I doubt if it's wide enough for two.'

'He won't notice me until you've gone, if I sit back there out of sight. I couldn't see you when I first came in. I don't suppose they'll realise what's happened until they come for you—tomorrow—and find me here instead. I think,' she said with eager excitement, 'I shall enjoy watching their faces.'

He realised at last that she was indeed in deadly

earnest, and all laughter left him. His expression was grave now, his tone unrelenting.

'No, mistress. It is out of the question. As you reminded me once, I have used the grief and suffering of others to my own advantage. Faced with death, I can see that, and acknowledge it. But I will not do it again. I will not, cannot, buy my life at the cost of yours. For that is what it would mean if you were to do this for me. They would know at once you were my accomplice, and if they did not hang you in my place you would be shut up here for God knows how long. And the gaol fever kills as many—more perhaps—than the gallows. I had it and lived, but many don't. I am sorry, but it would not do.'

'I am not afraid for myself—I want it for you!'

'Please let him accept,' she thought. 'If he loves me even a little he will know why I ask it of him, and he will say yes, surely he will.'

But he shook his head, calm, grave and immovable.

'No, Mistress Halsey. I cannot do it.'

What could she say? She stood helplessly looking at him, feeling the cold hand of despair settle over her again. Yet—no, surely there was another, better way, that he could not reject.

'Wait a moment, let me think. Suppose you were to attack me, overpower me, take my clothes and make your escape, leaving me here?—I could pretend you had knocked me out, perhaps—then they would not blame me, only think I was your victim. Wouldn't that work? Wouldn't we both be free that way?'

She could see that this time he was giving her plea some consideration: life did still mean something to him then. She watched him intently, praying that he would take what she offered, trying to gauge from his frown of concentration which way his choice would fall. Then her hopes died as he shook his head once more.

'No, even that would not do. What if you died of cold sitting here, waiting through the night for them to find you? What if I really hurt you, trying to make it look as though I was at fault? I couldn't leave you like that, not knowing that everything would be well with you.'

In her grief that he should manage to find objections to every little ray of hope which she tried to let in upon his life, and hers, Deborah's patient temper gave way. Angrily she grasped his arms, and shook him, and exclaimed:

'Why must you be so stubborn? Once you would have taken what I offer whether I wanted it or no—you would not have let me stand here talking for one moment before you had overpowered me and gone. And now you stand there though I plead with you, cruel and obstinate and blind and hard. Don't you see? I want you to live. I don't want to see you hanged tomorrow. What sense is there in that, if there's any way out? I would risk anything for you, anything at all, and you will not even let me run the danger of a little chill. If there is any humanity left in you, try this way. Go in disguise, and leave me bound here. Perhaps it will fail, perhaps they'll find out—if they hang me too I shall not mind—it would be better than not to have tried. Oh, if only you would believe I mean it, every word!'

'But how could I live with it afterwards, if you were to die, saving me? And that after all I've done to you already?'

She shook him furiously.

'Stop thinking of yourself and your precious conscience and self-respect, and think of me, and of what you need here and now! Do you want to die? Do you want me to watch you hang? Is that it; will your conscience be happy then? No harm will come to me if you do as I say, don't you see that? The worst I risk is a cold, and to

me that is nothing against your life. Please, by all you
hold dear, and for my sake!'

He said nothing for a moment or two, but this time
she saw from the look in his eyes—a mingling of hope,
reluctance, excitement—that she had won. She did not
relax, though, until she had his reply.

'I still cannot think it is right for me to agree—but
very well. I wish I was sure that I was right to do it.'

She laughed now, and her hands moved swiftly to
unclasp her cloak.

'Of course you are right. Quick now, we must not be
found before we are ready.'

She threw the cloak aside, and without a moment's
modest hesitation pulled off her stockings.

'Here, these will do to bind me.'

He took them, but there was no answering excitement, no enjoyment of the plan, in his expression.
Every move was slow, reluctant, full of repugnance at
what he was doing to her.

'You keep your back to the door,' she went on, 'then I
can see if the gaoler comes. We'll have to think of
something quickly if he does—Here, help me with this
lacing, then you can have my gown. Don't look like
that, I have a very respectable shift underneath—Now,
quick, quick, put them on and then you must bind
me——'

His slowness was painful to her, anxious as she was;
and she wished his enthusiasm and hope would match
hers. She helped him into the gown—much too short.

'You'll have to bend your knees,' she advised with a
laugh, and then tied the cloak about him. 'Now, I'll sit
over there, where you were, under the window. It's the
darkest spot—Don't just stand there. We've so nearly
succeeded.'

His face was grim as he tied the stockings about her,
and she laughed at his gentleness.

'They wouldn't hold a kitten,' she teased him. 'The gaoler will never believe my tale.'

'Then he'll have to disbelieve it,' said the Captain sharply. 'I cannot do anything to hurt you.'

His hands worked on, gently tying the inadequate knots.

'I can never repay you for this, because there is no hope we shall ever meet again,' he said. 'Yet if there were, I do not know what gift would be great enough to repay what you have given.'

'Your love,' she thought, 'that is all, and more than enough.' But at the same time she rebuked herself for her foolishness, and said lightly:

'What will you do when you leave here? Where will you go?'

'To the coast, I suppose. There are ports where loyal men can be found. And I shall find a ship to go overseas.'

'When I was a little girl in London,' she told him inconsequentially, 'I used to watch the big ships on the Thames, sailing away, and I used to feel that my spirit went with them, to all the freedom and happiness I could ever know. Perhaps it was the sails, shining and spreading in the sun, like silver angels' wings. Or the way they moved, so quiet, so smoothly on the water, like great swans.' She glanced up at him a little sheepishly. 'I suppose it was very foolish of me, a child's fancy.'

'A very pretty one,' he said lightly, though she sensed the unhappiness still there in him. He could not like what he was doing, however much closer it brought him to freedom.

He was ready at last and straightened, looking down at her. 'How can I . . .' he began awkwardly. 'I want . . . if only . . .'

And then they heard the approaching footsteps.

'Hush!' she urged. 'I think someone's coming. Pretend to weep, it's the best disguise.'

He tied the last knot swiftly, and then rose to his feet. He was by the door when the gaoler entered, a hunched and stooping figure sniffing into a handkerchief. Deborah lay still, and prayed that the man could not see her in the dark.

'Time's up,' said the gaoler. 'Here, he's not worth those tears. Out with you now.'

Disguise or not, Deborah could not bear to close her eyes as they left her. She watched every moment of his going, that unrecognisable grey-clad figure following the gaoler from the cell. And then the door clanged shut, the sound echoing along the passage outside, and she heard the footsteps receding; the heavy booted feet, solid and incisive, of the gaoler, and the shuffling uncertainty of his companion's feet. Then, distantly, another door rattled and banged and clattered shut, and she was alone in the haunted silence of the cell.

It was a strange night she passed there. It was bitterly cold, the stars pricked out with diamond clarity in the little patch of night sky visible through the window, the breath of air which reached her sharp with frost. She could not make any pretence of being comfortable, lying on the stone ledge which was the only seat, keeping still so that if they came in suddenly they would believe her story.

Slowly the chill crept into her limbs, her bones, she was cramped and stiff and frozen. Yet if she had not been so cold she would have slept, a deep and peaceful sleep of contentment and gratitude, the first she had known for weeks. With every slow hour which passed her happiness grew, for the plan had not been discovered and Captain Black had escaped.

She wanted to weep and laugh at once for joy in his safety. She knew now she could endure anything, any

misery her aunt chose to inflict upon her, with that
knowledge hugged to her heart.

'I, Deborah Halsey,' she thought, 'have saved the life
of the only man I shall ever love. He cares no more for
me than for any other soul he finds worthy of pity, but
perhaps he will always remember me for this one thing.
Perhaps, too, he will know that I did it for love, and the
thought will please and content him in the years to
come. I will never feel his arms about me ever again,
and I did not have that happiness today. I did not ask
all the questions I longed to ask, or tell him all I wanted
to say. But I shall have his memory always in my heart,
and there will be the less pain in it because somewhere,
because of me, he is alive.'

It was very odd to lie in that prison, shivering and
aching, and with such happiness deep inside her that
she longed to sing out loud.

Even so it was a long time until the dawn light slowly
seeped into the cell, and by then the numbness of her
limbs had reached even that secret core of happiness
and she simply lay there, barely conscious of why she
was there, or how she had come to this, waiting for
whatever the new day should bring.

Once the daylight had come she did not have long to
wait. She heard steps, far distant and faint, and then
that clanging door, and the steps louder and
nearer—two people, she thought. And then they were
just outside and she heard one of them speak in a low
voice, and the key turned in the lock. Two men, the
gaoler and another man who was clearly a chaplain,
came in.

The lantern they carried dispelled the last of the dark
and lit her recumbent figure. It was not difficult for her
to look as if some violence had been done to her. As they
exclaimed and came closer, their faces full of astonishment and horror, she shuffled slowly and awkwardly to

a sitting position, eyes half-closed against the glare of the light.

'He hit me ... on the head ...' she said unsteadily. 'He took my clothes ...'

The gaoler was swearing volubly; the chaplain, as befitted his cloth, gave a more restrained exclamation and came quickly to her side, his agitated fingers struggling with the knots.

'My poor child—what kind of heartless villain is it that could do this to you? I know he was hardened in wickedness, his heart closed to any godly exhortation—but this; this is too much.'

Shivering without any difficulty, Deborah added a few effective sobs. The chaplain removed his cloak and laid it about her. The gaoler, more concerned with the possible repercussions on himself of the prisoner's escape, asked sharply:

'Was that him then—in the grey cloak, that I let out last night? Was it you who came to see him just before dusk—?'

Deborah nodded, accepting the chaplain's proffered handkerchief and holding it to her nose.

The gaoler swore again, and laid down the lantern. 'I'm going for help—we must be after him——'

The words had no terror for Deborah: the Captain had been gone all night, and might even be at the coast by now. She dabbed her eyes to hide the triumph in them. The chaplain bent to raise her to her feet.

'Let's get you to a fire,' he said. 'You're half frozen, poor child.' He stooped to retrieve the lantern, and led her out of the cell and along the passage to a small guard-room, warmed by a roaring fire. He placed her in a large armchair before it.

'A hot posset, I think. Now, let me see——' He bustled about, assembling the necessary ingredients for the drink while Deborah sniffed into the handkerchief and felt the warmth return slowly and painfully to her body.

'Who are you? What made you visit that villain last night?'

'He's my half-brother,' sobbed Deborah. 'I hoped to bring him to repentance before his death.' The lie came easily, and she was unrepentant that at last she was able to lie for him. She had suddenly become very good at it. For his sake she could do anything.

The chaplain clicked his tongue.

'And this is how he repaid such concern for his soul! For that he must be beyond salvation—but you will have your reward, my child. Let us hope, too, that they find him—At what time did he leave? At dusk, did I hear?'

She nodded, and he pursed his lips. 'Not very good. He's had too long to get away. But we shall see. Here, drink this now—it's good and hot.'

Deborah sipped the hot drink, enjoying it the more because she felt it was taken under false pretences. The increasing warmth revived the joy within her, and it was difficult not to let it show.

'I do hope they catch him,' she said shamelessly, with a little quiver in her voice which her companion put down to distress, but which in reality sprang from barely subdued laughter. 'I'm so happy,' said that little voice inside her. 'He is safe!'

And then as the last of the cramping cold left her, and the fiery drink found its way round her body, her only remaining need reasserted itself. A half-wakeful night in a barn, a long walk and ride; a bitter chilling night—and now warmth, and comfort, and the contentment of a successfully accomplished mission. At ease in the chair Deborah fell, slowly, fast asleep.

The chaplain covered her with a blanket, and sat down with a book to wait for whatever might happen next. It had been a disappointing morning, for he had prepared a fine exhortation to inflict on the condemned man. Now it would have to wait for the next criminal to be led to the gallows—and very likely would need alteration before it could be used again. Fortunately such disappointments were rare.

Deborah had slept for several hours when two men returning empty-handed from the search for the escaped prisoner made a noisy entrance into the little room. She stirred slowly into wakefulness, for a moment fearing the worst, and her eyes focused thankfully on their anxious and disappointed faces.

Despite the chaplain's protest that she needed more rest and food, they bombarded her with questions: where might the Captain have gone, did she know? Who were the friends who might help him? Had he said anything to her last night which might give them a clue as to his whereabouts?

In her sleepy state it was not so easy to keep up the pretence, but with an effort she feigned regret and told them she had not seen her half-brother since they were children, for she had been brought up away from him, and had only sought him out again when she heard of his fate. He had always been wild, and mixed with bad company, she said: there had been friends in Leicester, she thought—that seemed safe enough, since she was fairly sure it was not near the sea. But she was very sorry, there was nothing useful she could tell them.

With that they left her in peace, and the chaplain went in search of food for her.

And then came the question she ought to have expected, but in all her careful loving planning had not thought of it at all.

'We'd better be getting you home, then. Where do you come from?'

Her stomach turned: what should she say? If she told

them to take her to Pembridge Hall, her real connection with the escaped prisoner would surely be revealed at once. Perhaps that would even lead them to guess at the truth about his escape. And in any case, how would she ever explain it all to her aunt without betraying those feelings too deeply held to be displayed before such insensitive eyes?

Then she remembered: 'If ever you need a friend, send for me.' She could not send for Robert Fanshawe, but she did need his friendship now, more perhaps than she had ever done.

'I live with my full brother, Master Robert Fanshawe, minister of Pembridge,' she said in a small pathetic voice. 'I should be very glad to be taken home.'

If he used her name, she could pretend it was a married name, she thought. But he was discreet, and knew her difficult situation, and might well be cautious before he gave anything away. It was the only solution she could think of.

So they found her a spare cloak and a place on a carrier's cart, and she set out in the company of the chaplain on the long jolting journey back to Pembridge, apprehensive, but knowing that nothing could destroy all her happiness.

As the journey progressed, Deborah began to suspect that she had indeed fallen victim to the one risk in the planned escape which she had regarded as trivial: she had caught a chill.

Under the heavy folds of the borrowed cloak she was first too hot, then shivering violently with cold. The Chaplain's talk—slow and infrequent though it was—reached her only vaguely, as if from a great distance, and often she would realise suddenly that he had spoken and she had not heard a word. By the time they came within sight of Pembridge she no longer felt warm at all, just a miserably shivering bundle of aching bones and throbbing head, unsure whether darkness was falling or whether she was simply no longer able to see well. She had never been so glad to see anyone as she was when Robert Fanshawe answered his housekeeper's summons at the front door of his little house, and came to the cart to greet her.

'Deborah! What are you doing? What has happened?'

One thought only shot through her fuddled brain, and she said unsteadily, 'Can't tell you now—brother.'

It sounded forced and unnatural, but fortunately it was enough. Robert took the hint and tried to hide his bewilderment and help the chaplain to lift her down from the cart.

'Bring her into the hall while I have her bed warmed,' Robert advised, acting his part smoothly and without hesitation. 'And then when we've made her comfortable you can tell me what accident has come to my sister.'

It was an enormous relief to Deborah to be laid, surrounded by cushions and covered with a blanket, on the settle by the wide hearth in the hall. Robert left the new arrivals for a moment then, ostensibly to give his orders to the housekeeper, and then returned to see what he could learn from the chaplain.

He knew that Deborah had run away: a distraught and furious Susan Foster had summoned him before church on Sunday morning expressly to tell him what she would do to her erring niece when she was found. Robert, suspecting a good deal more than Deborah's guardians would ever know, thought he could guess where she had gone, but he feared very much that she would reach Maidstone too late, or not at all, and his heart ached for what she must suffer there. And now here she was, half-dressed and feverish, barely conscious, brought to his house by a clerical gentleman he did not know, and he was entirely at a loss to understand it.

It did not take long, however, for the chaplain to tell him the whole story as he knew it. Robert listened attentively, taking note of the tale Deborah had invented so that he should do nothing to contradict it. He was able, too, he thought, to see what had really happened. Sympathetically, he imagined poor Deborah arriving, close to exhaustion, at Maidstone, a long and difficult journey behind her. She had bribed the gaoler, moving heaven and earth for that last meeting with the man who, in spite of everything, it seemed she loved. And Robert, who had felt sure that the man, for all his charm and striking good looks, was quite unworthy of the first devotion of Deborah's loving heart, felt a rising anger within himself that he should have been proved so distressingly right.

What kind of man was he who, faced with that love, could use it roughly, do violence to it to bring about his own safety? He had to keep a tight check on himself not to show more fury than a brother might show for a beloved sister so harshly used; but his protective instinct towards Deborah was strong, and he gave nothing away.

It was fortunate that the chaplain was anxious to leave quickly, hoping to cover at least half his return journey before nightfall. Robert was able to let him borrow a horse. Then Deborah must be taken to her uncle's house as quickly as possible, before she grew worse—she needed proper care, Robert thought, and good nursing. He hoped her aunt would relent enough to see that she had it.

He sat down for a few moments to set himself to work out a plausible story to account for her absence: she had run away because of her guardian's ill-treatment and been found wandering ill and half-clad some miles away, having been robbed on her journey. That should do, and prevent any awkward questions.

He hitched his remaining horse to the cart he kept for general transport about his small property, and as soon as it grew dark laid Deborah, well-wrapped, on the cart and drove across the village to the Hall, unobserved by any of his parishioners.

Deborah grew worse in the night. Her aunt, foiled in her intention to punish her niece for this new disgrace brought on the household, did her duty without warmth or enthusiasm, coldly ministering to the girl's needs, but no more.

It was fortunate perhaps that she never lingered long enough at the bedside to hear her niece's ravings, calling out despairingly to the man she loved, reliving again those days when she had thought he would die, muttering in feverish excitement her pleasure in his escape, and her part in it. If any of the servants left to watch her heard her words, they did not read any particular meaning into them.

Only Robert Fanshawe, when he came the next day, and the next, and waited at her side longing for some slight sign of improvement; only he knew what the words meant. He began to suspect uneasily that Deborah had not, after all, been simply the victim in the prisoner's escape. He could not be sure—did not even want to be—for it was a criminal offence to aid the flight of a condemned man. He tried to tell himself that whatever her feelings, she would not have gone so far; that she was too innocent, and the Captain too clearly a wicked man, for this suspicion to be true. But he felt that she could be forgiven any crime, if she would only live and grow well.

The fever left Deborah after three days, and she opened her eyes from the long healing sleep which had followed it to find her aunt standing at the bedside on one of her brief visits to the sickroom. She lay looking at that unsympathetic figure and wondered vaguely what she was doing there, trying to remember how she came to be in bed, in the afternoon, and what had brought her to this ridiculous state of weakness. She tried to gather sufficient strength to question her aunt, but Susan Foster cut her short to command Betty to bring broth for her niece, and then to leave her alone.

Betty told Deborah enough in answer to her feeble questioning for her to remember the rest; but it all seemed to have happened a very long time ago, to someone else. For the rest of the day she slept and woke alternately, took what food and drink they offered, and did not mind that for most of the time there was no one at her side.

By the next morning she could feel that her strength was returning, slowly but surely. She would have liked more company now, but was glad that at least no one asked her any questions; even more glad that her aunt, reassured that she would not die, did not come near her.

And then in the early afternoon Robert Fanshawe came to see her. He had heard of her recovery with immense relief, and the strength of it lit his expression as he entered the room. He had not been sure what to expect, though he had watched at many a sickbed in the past. He thought of the small figure lying flushed and restless and distressed in the great bed, and expected now to find the old Deborah sitting up to greet him.

She was still very far from sitting up, lying back against the pillows and looking, he thought, even worse without that hectic and unnatural colour and uncomfortable movement. She looked incredibly small and frail, the fine bones of her face stark beneath the near-transparent skin, the hair, very dark, spread round her on the pillow. Her eyes looked enormous in the thin face, almost black and deeply shadowed. But she had a warm and ready smile for him, and reached out one slender hand for him to take in his. It was, he thought, like holding a little bird in his great clasp.

'This is better,' he said with satisfaction, looking down at her with no trace in his expression of his anxiety about her. 'You will soon be about again, so your aunt says.' Though not too soon, if I can do anything to prevent it, he added to himself.

He had meant to talk to her of her escapade to set his mind at rest on the question of her part in it; to discuss her future, for it had been troubling him for a long time. But he could see that she had no strength as yet for anything but the most trivial talk, so he pulled a stool to the bedside and sat down and forced himself to engage in casual, cheerful, but suitably unexciting conversation. His visit brightened her day, and left her contented and ready to sleep.

He waited two days before he called again, and this time the change in Deborah was clearly marked. She was sitting up in bed—had even, she told him, been out of it for a little while that morning, and shape and colour were returning to her face. Robert waited until she had talked cheerfully to him for a little while, and then broached the subject uppermost on his mind.

'How much do you remember of the days before you were ill?' he asked.

The colour rose higher in her cheeks, and she looked down at her folded hands. 'All of it, I think,' she said, 'except that I'm not very sure of the last bit, when we came to your house.'

'You know then,' he said carefully, 'that Captain Black escaped from prison?'

'Yes.' Her voice was close to a whisper as she asked next: 'Did he . . .? Has he . . .?'

'He has not been recaptured,' said the minister, watching her closely.

She raised her head swiftly and smiled at him, with unmistakable joy. Robert felt suddenly depressed: a girl would not smile, surely, at the escape of a man who had deliberately attacked her—or would she? Could she love so much that she could forgive even that? He tried another approach.

'I could gladly throttle him for what he did to you. You went to him in all charity, and he abused your goodness—that is unpardonable.'

She frowned slightly, as if seeking the right words.

'It wasn't quite like that,' she said with caution. His eyes met hers, seeking the truth, and she blushed more deeply as he read it there.

'So I feared,' he said drily, and then explained, 'You talked in your fever.'

'Oh!' She looked dismayed. Who besides Robert had heard her?

'Don't worry. I think you would have to know half the story already to make any sense of it. Your secret is safe, but it's a dangerous one, Deborah.'

She smiled without the least sign of contrition.

'I know,' she admitted and then added: 'I'm sorry if it troubles you, but I thank you for your friendship. It has meant a great deal to me.'

It was his turn now, practical man though he was, to blush.

'It was not ...' he began awkwardly; and then tried again: 'I do not ... You ...' and then he gave up, with a helpless gesture of the hands. He decided upon a brisk change of subject.

'I promised you I would make enquiries,' he said, 'as to the terms upon which you may gain control of your inheritance.'

'And have you?' she asked.

'It took me some time; but, yes, I have found what I was looking for.'

'And?'

He looked at her gravely.

'I seem doomed to be the bearer of bad news,' he said. 'It seems your uncle has control of your fortune not until you come of age, as I had expected, but until such time as you marry. And even then, the control passes from him only if you marry with his consent. There is, I suppose, no need for me to remind you that once you are married your fortune passes entirely to your husband, barring whatever jointure the terms of the marriage settlement allow you.'

Deborah was silent for a little while, digesting the information.

'I don't think I'd ever hoped for anything more,' she said at last. 'I know you thought I should set up house somewhere by myself, but that never seemed any more than a pleasant kind of dream. It doesn't really matter. I don't care very much about money. I suppose it's only those who haven't got it who think it's important.'

'Perhaps,' he said. 'But I had hoped you might be able to use it to bring you freedom; even happiness.'

She smiled.

'It's kind of you to mind so much. I shall be all right, you mustn't worry about me.' She felt she could face anything the future might bring, now that she knew the man she loved was safe.

But her reassurance did not reach him: she wondered even if he had heard it.

'There is marriage, of course,' he began tentatively avoiding her eyes. 'A kind man, someone your uncle would approve of.'

'Now you know yourself that with the reputation I have no respectable man would marry me,' she said without visible resentment. 'And even if he would, it's not to say I could ever hope for my uncle's approval. But it doesn't matter,' she added swiftly, before he could make any comment, 'because I don't want to marry. I would rather go on here with things as they are, than that.'

That silenced him for some time, and when he spoke again it was to make some superficial comment on the weather. He did not stay much longer, and the rest of the time passed in meaningless talk.

By the time he left her Deborah was thoroughly puzzled, for though he had said nothing of importance at the end, there had been none of his usual smiles, none of the friendly warmth which she had come to expect from him. She had, in fact, a very clear impression that the idle conversation had been employed to hide something else, a serious anxiety, an emotion which for some reason he did not want to reveal.

But after wondering about it for a little while Deborah began to think she must have imagined it all, and he had been simply helping the time of her recovery to hang less heavy on her hands. It was good to have so comforting and dependable a friend. Even the future would not be so bleak with Robert Fanshawe's support and help behind her.

CHAPTER
ELEVEN

It seemed to Deborah only a very short time after the beginning of her recovery that life returned entirely to its previous pattern, and it was almost as if the adventure of the Captain's escape had never happened. As soon as she was strong enough—before that time, in Robert Fanshawe's opinion—she was reduced again to the daily round of drudgery and recrimination which had been all too familiar in the past. Her joy at the Captain's safety was reduced over the days to a tiny, almost imperceptible flicker of satisfaction, and the natural depression of the convalescent only made her face more clearly the realisation that he had gone from her life for ever.

It was over, and she found it very hard now to comfort herself with the thought that she had at least known what it was to love. Once or twice Betty or one of the other servants came on her weeping miserably in a corner of the dairy or the stable; more often she made sure that no one found her when she hid away to ease her despair at the awful dreariness of life without hope.

The one small piece of warmth and light in her existence was provided by Robert Fanshawe's steady friendship. It seemed as if he understood only too well what she was suffering, and was there with his sensible comfort when most she needed it. She did not realise that it was not only consolation he hoped to bring her, but some more lasting end to her hardships. He knew well enough that her guardians' treatment of her had made sure that everyone in the neighbourhood believed that the Captain had seduced her: knowing the truth, he set himself to work against the harshness of popular opinion, and show that he believed her innocent. That, as her minister, he should visit her, would have been natural enough whatever she had done. It would take more than that to build up her reputation again.

In the end it was his sister who gave him his opportunity, the sister from whose house he had been returning on the day he had first come on Deborah in the woods. She had been married for some years, and now at last her first longed-for child had been born. But the pregnancy late in her youth had left her weaker than she had expected, and the whole business of running the small farmhouse in which she lived with her husband, and helping with the work of the farm, had become too much for her. She had Nan to help, of course, but she and the hired man were the only other pairs of hands about the place. So Robert explained, with the air of one unburdening himself of his troubles, to Mistress Foster when he called one day in December.

'I really don't know where to turn to help her,' he went on. 'They can't afford to take on more servants about the place, and it doesn't help her to get well to know how much is not getting done for want of her work.'

'Have they no good neighbours to give a hand?' asked Susan, not greatly interested in the troubles of others.

'None who are free to do so,' Robert said, and then suddenly clapped his hand to his forehead in the manner of a man receiving inspiration. 'But of course, that would be a solution! Why didn't I think of it before?' He smiled amiably at the puzzled woman before him.

'Deborah,' he said, 'she is just the person. You do not keep her here because you need her work, but for her own good. Could you not spare her for a little while, just until my sister's more rested, to give a hand there?'

'But she is no fit person to take her place in the house of a respectable woman!' objected Deborah's aunt. 'That would be an insult to your sister.'

Robert forced himself to be patient.

'I think my sister's reputation is strong enough to take it,' he said firmly. 'And her need is so great that I am sure there could be no reasonable objection.'

It took some time, but in the end he won the argument. With great reluctance Henry and Susan Foster agreed that their niece should spend a week with the minister's sister.

For Deborah it was an idyllic seven days. She worked hard, as hard as she did at Pembridge, but there was no drudgery in it. It was an extraordinary sensation to receive effusive thanks and tearful gratitude for work which under her aunt's eye would have brought only wrath on her head. She had never known before what it was to be appreciated, and her starved spirit opened out like a flower.

Better still, she had pleasant company for every task. Nan was delighted to see her again, able for once to be able to talk easily and freely of everything she chose; and sometimes there was Robert's sister herself, a gentle kindly woman whom Deborah quickly grew to love. There were plentiful meals, fresh air, the freedom to walk when the day's work was done, the wonder of a new baby to rock in her arms; and above all the warming delight of friendship and laughter and affection. Deborah had not known such an existence was possible.

She had not known, either, that time could pass so heartbreakingly quickly as did that golden week. It seemed as if she had left Pembridge only yesterday

when Robert came riding up to the farmhouse to take
her back. It was the first time she had ever been less
than glad to see him.

The parting was warm and tearful, and Deborah left
with the music of their affectionate thanks ringing in
her ears and an ache in her heart. She rode a sturdy
pony at Robert's side, and it should have been an
enjoyable journey in the crisp brightness of the winter
morning with a friend for company. But the growing
dread at the thought of what awaited her at the
journey's end took all delight out of it.

It had been bad enough at Pembridge when she had
known nothing better; now, she knew, it would be
doubly hard to bear. Even in parting from the man she
loved, she had not been so strongly aware of the con-
trast with what she went to. Now she realised that even
without marriage, without the devoted love of a lifelong
partner, it was possible to be fulfilled and happy.

Robert, sensing her mood and grieving at having to
take her home—he had not realised until now how very
bleak her daily life had been—had little to say for the
early part of the ride. He could think of no suitable
words of comfort, nothing helpful which would not
seem unbelievably patronising from a man who had so
much more from life than Deborah had ever known.
But he watched her as they rode, hoping for some
opportunity to make things easier for her.

Deborah meanwhile was going over in her mind the
happiness of the past week, and remembering the darkness which went before; and slowly she began to see one
single, hopeful channel of escape. Now that she knew
that there were households where laughter and happiness could enliven the most humble task, she realised
that there was, after all, a way out for her even without
the fortune which her uncle controlled. Robert
Fanshawe, she was convinced, was the ideal person to

help her to take it. Her conclusion reached, she turned to him.

'You told me once you came from Rochester way,' she said. He looked surprised at an opening remark apparently so unrelated to what he knew must be troubling her.

'Yes, that's right,' he replied, 'I have an older brother who still lives there.'

'Then perhaps you know some families who might be in need of a servant?'

'I know several families very well,' he admitted, observing her closely, 'but whether or not any of them have need of servants I couldn't tell.'

'No, but you could find out,' she pursued. He drew rein and said slowly:

'Deborah, what are you trying to say?'

She followed his example and halted her pony beside him.

'Only that I think I could be quite happy if I could serve in some such household as your sister's, where people are kind and gentle and pleased if only one has done one's best to do right.'

She was amazed at the mingled pain and anger in his eyes.

'No!' he exclaimed. 'How can you even think of it? Why should you, an heiress of great fortune, a girl of good birth, go as a servant in some lesser man's house? That would be an indignity I could not allow you to inflict upon yourself—still less help you to do it.'

'You cannot think I should be worse off like that! After all, what am I now but a servant? Only worse than that, because I think even my uncle's servants are more kindly used than I am. And now I'm fallen so low I am no good for anything else. I cannot go and set up my own establishment, not having control of my fortune—you told me that—but to be a servant in some good household would be better far than that. This last week has shown me the truth of it.'

'It was meant to show the world that I did not regard you as below contempt, and nor did my sister,' was his rejoinder.

'Was it?' she asked in surprise. 'That was kind of you. And perhaps that will make some good man or woman the more ready to take me into their household.'

'It might, if I had any intention of helping you,' he said, and suddenly dug his heels into his horse's flanks, as if the discussion was over as far as he was concerned. 'Let's take the road past the castle where I met you that day.'

Deborah felt irritated that he could so lightly dismiss her argument, as if he could not even for a moment entertain the idea that it offered any solution. After all, it was she who had to endure the long days in her uncle's house, and surely she should be allowed to choose another way of life if it offered her some hope of happiness? And she was quite sure that it could. But she could not shout all that after him along the road, and he was already well ahead of her. She urged on her pony and followed him into the woods.

Robert rode quickly, as if he sensed that she would not otherwise let him rest, and Deborah's pony was too old and short of leg to keep pace with the minister's big brown horse. She would have liked to go more slowly past the castle, but Robert rode on and up the hill beyond without pausing, and not until they were again in the woods over the brow did he halt for her to catch up. She came slowly towards him, ready to plead for his help again as soon as she reached him, and then her eye was caught suddenly by a gleam of scarlet amongst the dead leaves beside the track, and she drew rein sharply.

'What is it?' called Robert.

Deborah said nothing, but slid from the saddle and

pushed aside the leaves to retrieve what lay there. In her hand Robert saw a limp piece of scarlet fabric, sodden and muddied but with the silver threads still visible along its border. He rode over to take a closer look.

'A gentleman's sash, I should think,' he said thoughtfully, 'of the kind worn with a sword. I wonder how it came there?'

And then he saw her face, white and wide-eyed, gazing at the stained silk as if she saw not that but something else, something of far greater significance. She seemed to have forgotten about him altogether.

She made no comment on his remark, but after a moment began to look slowly about her, and then to walk among the trees, turning this way and that, pausing now and then to examine a scarred tree-trunk or study some mark upon the ground. He watched her in bewilderment, wondering if she had gone out of her mind.

She remembered him at last, and looked up at him with an odd, excited light in her eyes.

'Can we go back and have a look at the castle?' she asked. He did not need great powers of perception to realise that her sudden interest was more than casual.

'Deborah, what's the matter? What is there about that rag that's so special?' For she was holding it to her as if it was some holy relic instead of a trivial piece of litter left by some careless passer-by. At his question she blushed deeply.

'I know what it is, you see,' she admitted, 'I knew as soon as I saw it. You're right, it is a gentleman's sash. But it is the one Captain Black used to blindfold me when I was his prisoner.'

'It is? Are you sure?' He looked at it with greater interest. 'But how did it get here?'

She told him how the dragoons had come on them in

the wood, and how she had been thrust aside and had pulled off the blindfold to see better. 'You can tell it was here they found us—see, on this tree, the marks where a musket-ball caught it—I found one too—just there, see. And here, see how this shrub is crushed and broken where the horses have stumbled over it. I know we came uphill from the place where they held me.' She paused to let the significance of the words sink in. 'So you see, I want to go down to the castle and look about there.'

Robert frowned.

'Won't that be rather painful? Wouldn't it be better to let it rest, to forget all about it?'

'No,' she replied gravely. 'That is something I can never forget as long as I live. If you don't wish to come there with me, stay here. I'll be as quick as I can.' She turned to remount her pony.

'If you must be so foolish, then at least it will be in my company,' he said with resolution.

They rode out of the trees and slowly down the long slope to the castle resting on its motionless lake. It was lovely still, even with the trees bare round it, the low slanting sunlight bright on its honey-coloured walls and weed-grown garden. They paused beside the lake and gazed at it in silence, and then Deborah moved her pony on to the worn drawbridge. Yes, that was the sound the hooves had made at the end of that first nightmare ride, and when they had set out in the dawn before the dragoons came. Afterwards, too, the short stretch of turf, the stone flags of path and courtyard—it all fitted. She dismounted then, and left the pony and Robert waiting there, watching her intently; and walked about, searching for the proof that would give her certainty.

She found the stables first, half-ruined, but with a number of stalls beyond the rubble still intact, and with clear signs that they had been used far more recently than the fall of the castle. Then, at last, she came on what she had been looking for all along: a low door, under an arched lintel, half-hidden by a heavy growth of creeper. It stood half open, the lock forced and hanging broken against the heavy wood. She pushed it gently, and it creaked wider. Beyond, a flight of steps led down, into darkness.

Unafraid, she went down, slowly, feeling her way. The smell was familiar, though it was more redolent now of damp and disuse than she remembered. At the foot of the stairs she stood still while her eyes grew accustomed to the feeble light from that concealed window, and then looked about her.

There was no longer any doubt. Mould and dust had spread over the sparse furnishings, and clearly the place had been searched at some time with ruthless thoroughness, the mattress tossed off the bed, its cover slashed, the table overturned. But there indeed she had lain and watched the men eating, talking, at cards; there she had spent the dreadful night hours; there, above all, been held for the only time in her life in the passionate embrace of the man she loved.

She stood there for a very long time, reliving in memory the days she had passed here: the fleeting smile, the lines of his face in the candlelight, the warmth of his arms about her, the passion of his kiss. She had been happy last week at the farm, but that was the commonplace happiness, new though it was to her, of an orderly, secure existence. The love she treasured within her, which had sprung into life in this place, was something rare and wonderful even to those who were used to the contentment so alien to her.

And now he had gone, and she had only the memory to bring back a little shadow of what had been, and the emptiness of knowing his arms would never fold about her again. She raised the sash to her face, oblivious of the smell of dead leaves and dampness, and tried to recapture something more, a deeper sense of what she had felt in his arms. But it was all in vain. He had gone and she was alone, and even if she succeeded in finding a happier way of life, she would never again love another human being as she loved him. That was over for her now.

She turned at last and slowly retraced her steps. She would come here again if she could, she promised herself, because she could feel at least a little closer to him, in this place where her spirit had taken fire: the place of which only she knew the secret.

Robert, worried at her long absence, had tethered the horses and come in search of her. She met him standing looking anxiously about him just beyond the concealing creeper, and he turned with an expression of great relief as she reached his side.

'I was afraid you'd come to some harm,' he said. He looked at her closely for a moment or two. 'Have you found what you wanted?'

'Yes,' she replied in a soft tone. 'It was here that I was shut up, that time.'

'Where? Behind there?' He indicated the doorway.

'Yes. Let's go now,' she went on quickly, because she did not want him to go and see it for himself. It would be an intrusion for anyone else to go there at this time.

She led him on, along the path and round the corner to where the horses waited, and there, suddenly, he reached out a hand and caught at her arm. 'Deborah, wait a moment.'

She paused, and turned to look at him. 'There is something I want to say to you.'

She smiled a little absently.

'Yes?'

'It is something I have wanted to say for a long time,'

he continued, and the gravity of his tone made her stand quite still, her eyes on his face, waiting to hear what he had to say.

Yet now that he had her attention he seemed unable for some little while to find the words he had felt so important. When at last he spoke he seemed to be returning to that contentious question of her future.

'Just now, when you asked me to help you find a place as a servant, I was not very willing to give you that help.'

'Not at all willing,' she corrected him, with a slightly acid note.

'It was not because I did not think it would give you a greater chance of happiness than you have at present,' he said next, 'but for quite another reason.' Again the words seemed to have deserted him, and she looked up at him impatiently.

'What was the reason?' she prompted him eventually. He bent his head now, so that he did not meet her gaze.

'Only,' he said very slowly, 'that I thought ... I hoped ... there might be another solution.' And then his head was up, and his eyes on hers, and the words flowed in a sudden torrent.

'Deborah, I think I have loved you since I first saw you, just up there that day in the autumn. I have tried to be your friend, to think what is best for you and try to do it, to help you in every little way I can without troubling you with what I felt. I knew very early after you came home what you felt for that—that Captain Black. I understand how you feel for you had never been in love, I imagine, and he was a fine-looking man, and charming too—No,' he held up his hand as she seemed about to protest, 'don't say anything. I'm not trying to belittle your love. I know it was real enough, so strong in fact that you broke the law to help him, and I know you love him still—I've seen that today. I don't ask you to love me, or to see in me any more than a friend. I think that one day you will realise that your Captain was not the man you once thought him, that there are qualities more important in a man than a fine figure and a smooth manner. If you had ever been in a position to marry him, I think you would have been very unhappy, once the first bloom had worn off—you are much too good for him——'

'You don't know him!' she broke in sharply, her interest in Robert's feelings temporarily quite overturned.

'No, but I have lived longer than you and know something of the world—it doesn't matter, anyway. He has gone, and it is all over. It is you who must be considered. I love you, and I would give you all I have and all I am, if you would have them. But I know it's too much to ask at present. One day, perhaps, when time has brought healing, but not now. Now I offer you only friendship, affection, security, contentment. If you will marry me, then these at least you will have, and you will find they are worth more in the end than the fickle passion of a penniless charmer. Will you be my wife?'

Deborah was so utterly astonished, so amazed that he should feel as he did, so overwhelmed with the realisation that he was not simply the comfortable friend she had thought him, but a man of deep unsuspected feelings, who wanted to make her his wife; that she stood rooted to the spot and quite unable to think of anything to say. The incredible, humbling thought went through her head that for the first time in her life someone thought her worthy of love. But she did not know how to reply.

'Deborah,' he said at last, in anguished uncertainty, 'what do you say? Will you marry me?'

That brought her back to reality, to face the truth of

her own feelings in this new situation.

'I can never love you,' she said with conviction.

'I didn't ask for your love,' he reminded her.

'No, but would you take me knowing you would never have it?'

'Yes, or I should not have asked. I hope—believe, even—that your feelings will change; but I know I cannot expect it.'

She fell silent again. She was moved by the generosity of what he offered, however little she might like his reflections on Captain Black's character. And she did not undervalue it either. She knew he could give her those things he promised, the kind of everyday happiness she had just left behind her, and she knew they would mean a great deal to her—after all, she had been ready to go as a servant to find them. In marrying Robert she would have more than that, too: a home and a partner for life, children most probably, a position of respect in the village community, a measure of responsibility in the household.

And as for him, what would he gain from the bargain? Precious little, as far as she could see: she wondered if he had realised that.

'It will do you no good to take me as your wife, with my reputation,' she pointed out.

'As my wife you will find it quite easy to remove any stain on your reputation,' he returned.

'And what if my uncle did not give his consent?'

'He would if he knew you would leave your fortune behind when you left his house.'

'And you think that is what I should do?'

'I would not suggest it if you had not assured me how little it meant to you. But it is you I want, not your fortune, and I would be happy that it should all go to your uncle if that meant you would become my wife. We would not be wealthy, of course—I am not poor, but not far from it either. But I think I am right in believing that you would not mind.'

'No,' she admitted, 'I would not mind. If, that is, I thought—if I thought it right for us to marry.'

'You would have a true friend at your side through all that life could bring,' he urged gently, and reached out to take her hand in his. She saw the pleading expression of his eyes, and knew what her answer would mean to him, one way or another.

But it was that last sentence, that reminder that he was ready to be her lifelong partner, which decided her. Every day, if she married him, it would be his face that she would see across the table, every night his head beside hers on the pillow. Her children would be his, his would be the only arms to embrace her, the only lips to meet hers with passion. And she knew she could not bear it. She knew that always, as long as she lived, there would be the memory of another man's arms, another man's kisses, to haunt her. She would ache with the longing to see that other man's likeness in her children, to turn and see his eyes meet hers at the shared moments of joy and sadness. Robert had not asked for her love, but she could not vow to give him all of herself knowing that she could not do it, ever.

Yet as she laid her free hand over his strong brown one, she grieved for the pain she must cause him.

'I am sorry, but I cannot be your wife,' she said; knowing that in saying 'no' to a future at his side, she was at the same time accepting a future without his friendship. For how, after this, could they ever again meet with the easy affection which had meant so much to her?

CHAPTER
TWELVE

THE winter that year was a harsh one and a long one, as far as Deborah was concerned. She returned to the cruel routine of life in her uncle's house knowing at last that there was something better, even if it was not for her. And her hardships were not lightened now by the frequent visits of the minister. He came still, took prayers sometimes, talked with her aunt and uncle or the servants, even now and then with her. But when they met he was shy and awkward in manner, asking after her but unable to show his concern without remembering always what was between them. And Deborah could not ask for his help now that she had rejected the thing he had most wanted to give: her only wish was to spare him embarrassment and pain by seeing him as little as possible, however much it cost her.

So she endured as best she could, and tried to bring herself to some kind of acceptance of the fact that, as far as she could see, this was to be the pattern of her life for years to come. Constantly watched as she was, she could not set about trying to find a servant's post for herself: in any case, without a reference probably no respectable household would take her on. And she could not even hope for another short stay with Robert's sister to lessen the burden, for that was all in the past.

And then, with lengthening days and increasing sunlight and the first flowers opening, the spring came; and with it two changes which Deborah had not anticipated in her wildest moments. Her uncle died; and the exiled King Charles was restored to the throne of England.

The second change affected her very little, in fact she scarcely noticed it. She was aware of talk, and an air of excitement, and then of that exquisite spring day when the church bells rang until her head ached, and bonfires leapt up in celebration on every hill top and village green. But inevitably, in a house where Cromwell was held up for the general example, the return of the King could offer no possible excuse for rejoicing, and so news of the general gladness reached her only by hearsay, from the servants' chatter or chance-heard talk of passers by.

Even if they had been Royalists of the staunchest kind, they would have found it difficult to rejoice so soon after her uncle's death. He had died unexpectedly of a fever which had apparently begun as nothing more than a slight chill, and he had been ill for only two days when the end came.

Deborah could not mourn his loss, for she had known nothing from him but harshness; but she did not expect his going to make any difference to her. After all, it was her aunt who had stood over her and bullied her, and found fault with her, and whipped her from time to time. She had, on the whole, seen very little of her uncle.

But it did make a difference in a surprising way. It seemed that there must have been a deeper affection between husband and wife than anyone had ever guessed at, for Aunt Susan went completely to pieces at her Henry's death. She retained her calm and her dignity until the sombre duties of the funeral were over, and then she retired to her solitary room and shut herself in, and wept and would see no one for more than a week. Even Robert Fanshawe could not reach her.

When she emerged at last she was a changed woman.

She had never appeared to enjoy life, but now it did not seem to interest her at all. She was listless and easily tired, unconcerned if the work was not perfectly done, untroubled by signs of levity in the kitchens. In fact she often let whole days pass without penetrating at all to the working regions of the house. The effect on the servants was almost immediate and very marked. The work was done still, on the whole, though not always with a great deal of care, but the atmosphere in the kitchen was transformed. Laughter and talk flowed freely, food meant for the parlour was eaten before it reached so far, for Susan Foster had little appetite these days. Some even dared to be absent from household prayers.

And on Deborah the effect was perhaps greatest of all. Her aunt no longer subjected her to constant watchfulness and criticism. She had the same work to do as before, and now and then Aunt Susan would remind her of it, but she was able to do it as the other servants did, without subsequent comment. Sometimes she even found herself, for a little while, with nothing much to do. Gradually the silence which had surrounded her was broken down and her companions began to talk to her, to share their feelings and their jokes with her, to treat her as one of themselves. She had always been liked and lately, pitied, and now they were glad to be able to show it.

Without taking any deliberate step, without being faced with any irrevocable decision, Deborah found herself living something like the reasonably contented life for which she had longed. She even had a little freedom sometimes, now that her aunt no longer seemed to mind very much what she did, and once or twice she found her way to the castle and passed a few hours there, in that place which had become some sort of shrine to her lost love.

And then, as time went by, she found that the restoration of the King was also to have its small effect upon her. That it had affected some of the people she knew she had already realised. Sir Edward Biddulph had suddenly emerged in dazzlingly elaborate clothes and a substantial wig to conceal his sober hair, and very quickly married a girl whose Royalist father had recently recovered his substantial estates. Deborah pitied her.

Robert Fanshawe, on the other hand, was likely to lose his living as minister to Pembridge, just as the previous Royalist vicar had been turned out eight years ago to make way for the young Puritan clergyman. It was said, though, that a wealthy Cromwellian who owned large estates nearby was ready to take him on as his personal chaplain. He had three daughters, they said: Deborah hoped that one of them at least would be gentle and pretty and very ready to console Robert for what he had lost.

And then she began to find out that she too was not to be untouched by this other change. England, she soon realised, was now full of penniless or near-penniless Royalists, who had sold their lands to pay fines, and then found that long years of loyalty to their King did not ensure ample material rewards now he was safe on the throne. She began to think, even, that most of them must be concentrated in this part of Kent, for it took only a short time—a few weeks—before a continual stream of them began to appear at the door of Pembridge Hall.

To men used to the life of King Charles's court, Deborah Halsey's doubtful reputation was no handicap against the certainty of her considerable fortune. A rich wife was a sure means of restoring depleted estates, or financing a courtier's existence. Deborah regarded the first two or three with astonishment that they should show an interest in her, and then amusement at their very half-hearted attempt to hide their base motives; and then, after a time, she grew heartily weary of the whole business.

Unfortunately, one consequence of her aunt's indifference to her was that she no longer seemed to mind the thought of her niece's marriage. Perhaps the fortune had ceased to mean anything to her, now that she had no Henry to share it with. Deborah could almost have pitied her if her aunt had allowed her to express her thoughts on the matter. But for whatever reason, Susan Foster now seemed almost to look with favour on a marriage for Deborah. She began to show clear signs of disapproval, of a wish to have the girl off her hands as soon as possible.

'Time you had a household of your own,' she was even moved to say one day. It was clear that Deborah had become simply an irritating encumbrance.

It did not make life as miserable as before to know her aunt wanted her out of the house; but it made it all a little difficult to know what was to become of her if she could not somehow win Susan Foster's affection. Deborah pondered the problem a great deal, even discussed it with Betty, who had proved to be discreet as well as sympathetic.

'I thought once of going to be a servant in another house,' she said, as if it had been no more than a passing fancy. Betty looked shocked.

'Oh, I wouldn't do that! You never know, you might find yourself worse off than you are here, and not able to walk out of it. You never know.'

Deborah thought that as things now were, that might well be true. Perhaps, she reflected, if she approached her aunt at a suitable moment, she might induce her to let her take her fortune and go. But she did not know quite how one set about establishing a household without the help and friendship of someone like Robert Fanshawe.

So she let the days pass, and hoped that some natural solution would offer itself. Meanwhile she filled her increasing moments of spare time with the things she had enjoyed most in the past, on the rare occasions when she had been allowed to indulge in them. She worked at embroidery, a skill which Nan had taught her long ago; or on sunny days she wandered in the garden, pulling up a weed here and there, watering her favourite plants; or she gathered herbs and fragrant flowers and made experimental perfumes and medicines in the stillroom. It was not a very purposeful existence, but far from being an unhappy one.

And then one hot morning in July she was crossing the hall on her way to the garden after breakfast, leaving her aunt gazing out mournfully over the breakfast table, when she saw through the open door that a coach emblazoned with an impressive coat of arms had turned in at the gates of the Hall.

'Oh no! Another suitor!' was her immediate thought, and she fled up the stairs and shut herself in her room. There had been a lull lately, a whole two weeks without an offer of marriage, and she had hoped that was a sign that she was to be left in peace.

She was right. In about half an hour—clearly this one had given more time than usual to the preliminary courtesies to her aunt—Betty tapped gently on the door, and came in at Deborah's answering call.

'I know exactly what you're going to say,' said Deborah. 'And you know my answer, don't you?'

Betty smiled, and sat down on the stool Deborah indicated. 'Yes, I know——But this one's a lord!' she added impressively.

Deborah laughed.

'I don't care if he's the king himself,' she said. 'The.

answer's the same. I do not wish to marry.'

Betty put her head on one side, like a robin observing the oddities of human kind.

'He's very handsome,' she said, 'and he came in a coach.'

'I know,' returned Deborah, unrelenting. 'I saw it.'

'He wants to see you.'

'Then you will have to tell him I will not see him. And he must go away and find himself another rich spinster.'

'Won't you even see him? He's Lord Lenoyer, who used to own that ruined castle in the woods. He says he means to restore it and live there. That would be grand, to live in a castle!'

Deborah felt her heart miss a beat, and then quicken with dismay. She thought of her haven there, the unpromising little room in which all her most precious memories were concentrated. What would they do to it? She could not hope that they would leave it untouched; and even if they did it would be built over, hidden, no longer open for her to wander in, reliving the past. At that instant she hated Lord Lenoyer.

'I don't want to live in a castle,' she said in an angry biting tone which took Betty by surprise. 'He can find another rich wife to pay his builders: I am not available. Go and tell him to leave at once.'

Betty shrugged, and went.

But it seemed that Lord Lenoyer was obstinate, or stupid, for the maid returned within a few minutes with a small box of tooled leather clasped in her hand.

'He won't go. He sent this—a gift for you, he said.'

'Then you can take it back!' snapped Deborah in exasperation. It was not like her to be irritable, but she was thoroughly tired of these constant assaults on her peace of mind. 'I don't want him or his gifts.'

'I think he meant you to have it anyway,' said Betty

doubtfully. 'Won't you even look at it?'

Deborah saw the avid curiosity in her eyes, and relented a little.

'Very well. Just one look, then you can take it back.'

She lifted the lid, and looked in, and gave a gasp of delight. 'Oh, it's beautiful!'

Inside, nestled in the velvet lining, lay a tiny model of a ship, exquisitely fashioned in silver. Every detail of sail and rigging was carefully, accurately marked, every line of her hull perfectly fashioned, even to the elaborate decoration below the cabin windows and the beautiful miniature figurehead.

Betty looked at it with a slight frown of puzzlement.

'It is pretty,' she admitted, 'but what a funny present.'

'Yes,' said Deborah, glancing at her as if that had not occurred to her before, 'it is rather strange. I like it very much, though—but you are not to tell Lord Lenoyer that.' She closed the box with a snap, and handed it to Betty. 'Return it to him with my thanks, and my good wishes for his future without me.'

This time the tiresome suitor accepted his dismissal at last and drove away in his carriage, and Deborah heaved a sigh of relief at the sound of the departing vehicle. Halfway down the stairs she came face to face with Betty, and saw at once that the little box was still in her hand.

'I thought I told you to return that,' she said sharply.

'Yes,' said Betty uncomfortably, 'but when I gave it to him he looked rather unhappy, and he said "She can keep it—I don't want it", and then he went without any trouble. So here it is.'

Deborah took it in silence, and carried it to the safety of her room. She would have liked to stand the little ship at her bedside, so beautiful was it; but it reminded her too much at present of the importunity of its giver for her to enjoy looking at it for long. Later, when she had forgotten all about the persistent suitors, she would display it for all to see.

She had hoped that was the end of that little affair at least, but when she reached the hall she found that she was wrong. Her aunt was at that moment emerging from the parlour with a look of ill-temper on her face—it was unusual for her these days to show any emotion but grief, and Deborah's courage failed her a little. She guessed that the anger would be directed against her, for it always had been in the past. In the vain hope that it would not be this time, she forced a smile.

'Ah, Deborah,' her aunt spoke without warmth. 'I want to talk to you: come in here.'

Deborah followed her into the parlour with a sinking heart. Perhaps Susan Foster was beginning to overcome her grief, and would once more be directing her ruthless attention to every aspect of the household. Inside the room, Aunt Susan closed the door and turned to face her niece.

'You have just refused a very suitable offer of marriage,' she said at once, in a sharply accusing tone.

'Yes,' replied Deborah, with a lift of the head. 'I don't wish to marry.'

'But you must marry. Do you expect to go on living here for ever, always under my feet and in my way?'

'I try not to be in your way,' replied Deborah meekly.

'Then you don't succeed.' Susan Foster crossed to the fireside, her back to her niece. It was clear from her voice that she was near to tears. 'Henry never liked you: we were of one mind, he and I. I don't want to live with you always here, slinking about to remind me that my Henry died, and you are living still. What justice is there?'

Deborah felt slightly sick.

'I did not choose it,' she said faintly, and stumbled to a chair. She had known she was not liked; but it was horrible to think she was hated so much that her aunt could not bear to see her about the house.

'Why did you not accept Lord Lenoyer?' Mistress Foster went on. 'You could not have a more eligible suitor—a title and lands, all you could want.'

'It is not all I could want. I am not going to marry a man who wants only my money to keep him in comfort. A man who thinks any woman fit to marry, so long as she has wealth.'

'You should be thankful anyone does want to marry you, whatever the reason! You're not much of a proposition.'

'And whose fault is that?' thought Deborah, but she kept it to herself. 'I don't want a husband!' she said aloud, and with emphasis. 'Why can you not accept that?'

'Every woman wants a husband. Every woman needs one. And you cannot stay here.'

'Then let me go,' urged Deborah, impulsively seizing her opportunity. 'Help me to find somewhere to live, and good servants, and let me live there alone. That is all I ask, and it's not very much, surely, if it brings you what you want as well?'

'Do you think me fit to scour the countryside for somewhere for you to live, or root out servants, or set your life to rights for you? I am broken, Deborah, broken, without Henry at my side. Be warned, you will gain nothing if you try to live alone, only the final end to what reputation you have left. Only whores and actresses live like that.'

'Or widows,' thought Deborah: 'Perhaps I'd better find a very old husband.' Aloud, she exclaimed:

'Then what can I do?'

'Marry, of course! What have I been saying all along?

What if a man is after your money? That is what marriage is for—what could be more fitting than for a wealthy girl to marry a man with lands and a title who is in need of money? Then you have everything.'

'Except love,' said Deborah sadly.

'Love? What has love to do with it? That comes sometimes, but it is not what marriage is for. You don't know what you're talking about. It is your duty, as my niece, to show the respect due to your elders by obeying my wish that you should marry. Who you accept I leave, within reason, to you. But marry you must. That is not a request, but a command. And it must be soon, within the year—sooner if possible. If only you had not sent Lord Lenoyer away—but you can hardly call him back!'

'Nor do I wish to,' repeated Deborah, but she was helpless to assert her independence in any other way. She crossed to her aunt's side, and laid a hand on her shoulder. It was shaken off at once, with distaste, but Deborah persevered.

'Aunt Susan, could you not learn to like me just a little? I know I could love you too, if you would only let me. Perhaps my uncle did dislike me, and I know how deeply you grieve for him; but that doesn't mean you have to go on thinking and feeling exactly as he did for the rest of your life. I am your own flesh and blood, nearer to you than anyone in the world. My mother was your own sister: can that not move you to accept me in your house?'

Her aunt turned, with an odd light in her eyes.

'Yes, she was my sister. And do you know how it was all our lives until she married? I never had a moment's rest from torment while I was under the same roof with her. She was younger than me, but she had all her wits about her, and she knew how to charm. She teased and ill-treated me every day of our childhood, but no adult would ever believe she was at fault. It was always I who was punished, whatever she did. It was like that all her life. Everything she touched turned to gold. I knew there was no justice when she was the first to marry, and did so well for herself, catching that rich husband with his grand London house.

'Then she bore children, when I had none—true, her son died, and she was left with nothing but a girl, but it was more than I ever had. When she died I did my duty by you, and had you here, and it's as well you look nothing like her—except for that hair—or it would have been more than I could stand. But to see her chit of a daughter an heiress, with everything I never had—that was hard, very hard. And now I have nothing at all, and you stand there and ask me to love you. You have your answer: just leave me in peace, that's all I ask.'

Deborah turned and left the room with the weight of her aunt's jealousy and bitterness heavy on her shoulders. She looked about her as she went, carefully noting the signs of comfort, of a life far removed from poverty or want: the fine house, the good furniture, the pictures and curtains and blazing fires in every hearth. Had her aunt been so obsessed with envy of her sister that she had been blind to all she had herself, unable to enjoy it for longing for the few things she could not have? She did not even seem to have been glad that her marriage had brought her love, unaware of it perhaps until now when she had lost it, and it brought her only sadness.

Poor Aunt Susan! But Deborah knew it meant, as she had been told just now, that there could never be any affection between them. The bitterness had lasted too long.

She did not know what to do now, where to turn for help. Robert had gone from her life, and even if he had not she could no longer make use of him. Betty was too inexperienced to be able to do more than listen with sympathy; and there was no one else. She could not leave home and she could not stay. It seemed as if marriage was the only way out, and yet that was impossible. The thought of marrying Robert had been more than she could bear: to marry a stranger, interested only in her money, would be an obscenity too dreadful to contemplate. Yet what else could she do?

She sat for a long time at the window of her room, gazing out on the garden. Perhaps, she thought at last, a walk might help her to decide what to do, or at least to distract her from the impossible dilemma. The woods would be cool today, green and inviting, and——

She remembered suddenly what Betty had told her: the castle was to be restored. If Lord Lenoyer was already in the area, work must be about to begin all too soon. She had no time to lose if she was to go there once more before it was all alive with workmen.

She rose to her feet, and in a moment was crossing the sleepy sunlit garden on her way to the one place which was special to her alone.

CHAPTER
THIRTEEN

DEBORAH'S enjoyment of the woods was spoilt that day by the two anxieties uppermost in her mind: her concern about her own future, and her fear lest she should find that the seclusion of her sanctuary had been already invaded.

She had about a mile to go, and she walked on oblivious to the vibrant loveliness of the trees in all the rich fullness of their summer foliage, to the fragrant coolness where the green leaves shaded her from the intense sunlight.

On her first walk along this path she had looked about her with all the eager avidity of a newcomer: now she saw nothing at all. She had hoped that the walk might help her to reach a decision, but it did not seem to help at all, though she was glad of the excuse to keep moving—worries always seemed at their worst in moments of repose.

As she drew nearer to the brow of the hill where she knew she would have her first sight of the castle, she strained her ears for any sound of voices, or vehicles, or hammering. There was none, but until she saw for herself she could not be sure.

And then she was there, standing looking down on that secret valley, and she breathed a great sigh of relief. All was well. There was no one there, nothing stirring, not even the swan, no sound but the gentle movement of the leaves in the breath of air which was not quite a wind. She was alone.

And she thought it had never looked so breathtakingly lovely as it did now, the shadows plum-dark where the sun did not reach, the lake as motionless as if it were all a dream. As it had the first time she had seen it, the castle gave her the illusion of being whole, complete and perfect on its shining water.

She thought that in a way Betty had been right, and it would be good to live here; but not because of the grandeur of living in a castle. She could never have said what it was about this place which had caught at her heart long before it had any personal associations for her: she only knew she loved it, that it held some special secret magic for her alone, that if she were asked to describe her dream of Paradise, it would come somewhere near to the loveliness which lay before her.

And now, like Eve, she was to be shut out of Paradise for ever.

She smiled wryly at the thought that it could have been hers if she had acted differently that morning. But would she not then have found that there was a serpent at its heart to poison her happiness? A house, however beautiful, and a lake, and a valley lovely as a dream, would not be enough by themselves to make her happy. And there would be a kind of sacrilege in agreeing to share them, sacred as they were to her, with a man like Lord Lenoyer, a seasoned courtier with a cynical eye to his own advancement.

So today she must take her last farewell of this beautiful place, and carry her memory away to cheer her when life became most difficult. She would not come back again, ever.

She left the hilltop and walked slowly down. There was no thought now of her anxieties, for she wanted to imprint everything so firmly on her memory that nothing afterwards could wipe it out. She studied it as attentively as she had once gazed at the face of the man she loved in the candlelight, the only man with whom she would ever have wanted to share it all.

She saw as she came to the drawbridge that the swan was there after all, gliding smoothly beneath the towers at the far side of the castle. Like one of those proud ships she had watched on the Thames as a child, she thought, exquisite, magical, mysterious, hinting at a world of happiness and fulfilment she would never know. She stood looking at him for a little while, so coolly in-different to her as he was; and then she went on and across the drawbridge.

The dark underground room was much as it had always been, though the summer sun had dried it out a little. But today, somehow, it had lost its power to bring back the past for her. She stood there for a long time, but the memories eluded her: she smelt only the damp mustiness of it, saw only the grimy disorder. She strove to remember what had happened there, what she had felt, to recover something of the emotions of that last day.

And there was nothing, nothing at all. Her mind recalled what had been said and done, but she could no longer feel the reality of it. She felt a new desolation, at the thought that even this had been taken from her, and she turned and made her way slowly back, up the stairs, out into the sunlight.

Then she heard voices.

They were not very near, perhaps beyond the water, and she thought there were two, both men. Then there came the unmistakable sound of a snorting horse. Very slowly she crept along the path until she could peer round the broken end of the wall, and see them.

There were three men, and their horses. One, clearly a servant, stood a little apart, holding their mounts; the other two were deep in conversation at the point where the drawbridge reached the land. The one facing her was clearly some kind of businessman: an architect or builder, perhaps, and a prosperous one, well-dressed, with a parchment—some kind of plan, she supposed—clutched in his hand. The man with his back to her was talking at present, his arm gesturing in broad sweeps towards the castle. He was tall, slim, magnificently dressed, from his splendidly plumed hat to his elegant beribboned boots.

'Lord Lenoyer,' said her mind, instinctively. Clearly the castle's restored owner had come to discuss his rebuilding plans with the professional man who was to undertake the work.

She retreated out of sight behind the wall. What should she do? She did not see what else she could do but wait here until they went away. And hope that they did not stay too long. Or, worse still, venture across the drawbridge. She sat down on a fallen block of stone in the shade of the wall, and waited.

She had been there long enough for the heat to have made her drowsy, when she was roused sharply by the sound of approaching footsteps. They were coming, she thought, along the path, and in a moment would be here. She stood up, ready to run and hide.

Only one man came round the corner to where she was, and as her eyes reached his face she felt as though all her limbs turned to water.

The fair skin, the fine bones, the supple mouth; the dark eyes she remembered so well beneath the straight brows; the shining fairness of the hair beneath the wide-brimmed hat. Seeing her, he removed the hat and stood absolutely still, as she was, gazing at her in amazement.

'You!' she said faintly. 'It's you! How did you come here?'

She felt the joy begin to rise in her, the incredible, amazing joy that they should meet again like this. And then she saw his expression, and a chill settled over her heart.

There was no answering joy in his eyes, no light, not even the welcoming gentleness with which he had greeted her in the prison. She wondered if perhaps he did not know her, though it was he in his splendid clothes who looked different, not she. But why otherwise was his mouth set in that hard line, that frown etched above the dark brows?

'Don't ... don't you remember me?' she asked falteringly, though that was a ridiculous question: he could not forget, surely, in so short a time, that she had saved his life.

'Of course,' he said, so curtly, so without any warmth of emotion, that she felt dizzy at it. 'What are you doing here?' He spoke almost in the tone of a landowner confronting a trespasser.

'I—I come sometimes ... I found the place where ... where we were.' There was a great ugly lump in her throat and she could say no more.

Her eyes moved to where his slender hand lay upon the wall, clutching the stonework as if an intensity of emotion lay behind the grasp. Yet it was not there in his face or his voice.

'I'm surprised that it means anything to you,' he said coolly.

'How can you say that?' she returned indignantly. 'It is not so very long since I begged you to save your life—that I—Oh, what does it matter now?' she ended wearily, longing only to crawl away somewhere and weep that she had woken from her last dream, to find that now even that was ashes.

'Exactly,' he said. 'It doesn't matter. You made that clear this morning.'

Her eyes widened in surprise.

'This morning? What has this morning to do with it?'

She saw a slight, a very slight, softening of the hard line of his mouth, a little uncertainty in his eyes.

'I came to your house this morning to ask you to become my wife. Or have you forgotten that already? Clearly it meant very little to you.'

She stared at him blankly, uncomprehending.

'You? ... To ask me ...?' And then, slowly, she understood, with a choking leap of the heart. '*You* are Lord Lenoyer!'

The colour rose and flooded his face, and she saw that his hands were trembling.

'You did not know?' he asked with clear amazement.

'How could I know? I thought it was just one more man after my money.'

He steadied himself against the wall and paused to take a deep breath. Then he said: 'But the ship? Didn't that mean anything to you?'

She thought of it, the exquisite silver miniature, and understanding dawned. Of course: she had told him in the prison how she had loved to watch the ships, how they seemed to invite her to happiness. It had not been a strange gift but a key, a clue to tell her who it was who waited for her below. She was trembling now.

'I ... I did not realise,' she said. She raised her eyes to his face, and half-whispered: 'You asked me to marry you—— You must have thought I did not care.'

He raised his hand and pressed it for a moment to his dazed eyes, and then stared gravely at her, as if still he could not be sure what she felt.

'Then you ... do ... care?' he asked unsteadily. Her eyes held his.

'I shall love you as long as there is breath in my body,' she said, joy filling her that at last she could tell him without fear, without hesitation. And all the time the words sang in her head and in her heart: 'He asked me to marry him—he asked me to marry him——'

His hand still on the wall, as if now to still the trembling a little, he smiled down at her.

'I was foolish to leave it so much to chance. It was only that I did not want to betray our secret to your aunt.'

'She was very angry that I refused you.'

'And so she should be. Shall I call tomorrow and make her happy? Would your answer be different then?'

She laughed softly at the foolishness of the question, the obvious, the only answer on her lips. And then suddenly, chillingly, she realised why he had asked her to marry him. In her love and her joy at seeing him she had thought only that her love was returned, that every dream of happiness, every hope, everything she had ever wanted from life had come together at this moment, to a golden glowing reality.

But she remembered now what he had said when they had parted in the prison cell. 'I can never repay you for this——' 'I do not know what gift would be great enough——'

There had been no word of love, though he must have realised, surely, what had driven her to save his life. And recognising her love, he had it in his power now to repay the debt not with the love he did not, could not, feel, but with his title and his lands and everything he owned.

The light faded from her eyes, the colour from her face, and she gazed at him, stricken by her understanding of the truth.

'No,' she said faintly, shaking her head. 'My answer would be just the same.'

She could not take him on those terms, binding him to a mockery of a marriage in which she would never have his heart though she had everything else that was his. She could not bring that grief either on herself.

She saw the light die in his eyes, too, at her words. It mattered then, that he should repay his debt. His sense of honour demanded it, and he knew of nothing else he could offer her. But even so she could not accept the gift.

'Why not?' he asked, drily, his voice harsh, rasping.

She bent her head, to hide the tears in her eyes.

'Because if there is to be love at all it must be on both sides,' she said slowly, and so quietly that he could scarcely hear.

She heard him move, felt his fingers beneath her chin, tilting her head back until her eyes met his. His expression was grave, solemn, earnest.

'What makes you suppose that it is not on both sides?' he asked.

'Oh! ... I ...'

'Why do you think I decided to let you go when I had you here, my prisoner?' he went on quickly. 'I did not know what you felt for me, except that you said it was hate; but I knew from the moment when you showed me what I was—no, even before, perhaps—that I loved you, wanted you, as I'd never loved any woman before. I was angry that I could lose my heart so easily, so very inconveniently, but I was angry with myself, not with you.'

'So,' she broke in, 'you were taking me home when the soldiers came——?'

'Yes, did you not know?—I suppose I didn't tell you—But how could you not know, you foolish Deborah, that I loved you, that I could love no one, ever, but you? If I had not loved you I could not have taken what you offered in the prison. It was because I knew I would have had to do the same for you, if I had been in your place, that I could bring myself to use you like that.'

He laughed softly, as if some joy in him was too great

to contain, and then he reached out and took her hands in his. 'My dear blind little love, not to know that you have all my heart—and yet, my darling,' he went on in wonder, 'you gave me all that just the same, expecting nothing in return—— Oh, Deborah!'

She wanted to dance and sing and shout and weep, the joy bubbling over too great for common words, and she could only say, half-sobbing: 'I think it is all a miracle, that you should love me.'

He laughed too.

'Not a miracle, dear heart, but the only possible response to what you are—— No,' he went on, seeing her eyes widen with disbelief, 'I am serious, my darling. Believe me, I have travelled over hundreds of miles, I have been present at the courts of kings, yet I have never in all my life seen any woman who could match you in beauty. And yet you have more than that, far more. Qualities which no one would ever find among the pampered beauties of the court. You are gentle and modest, kind and simple-hearted, and yet you have the courage to speak out with indignation when you know wrong has been done. I took you prisoner, and you made me ashamed not only of what I did to you, but of nearly all I have ever done and of what I am. That, I could say, is why I, who have never loved another woman, lie now in the palm of this little hand'—he turned it upward, and kissed it gently—'entirely at your mercy. And yet it is not the whole story, for there is so much more I feel for you. It is only that there are not words enough to tell you of it.'

For a moment she closed her eyes, as if what he said had overwhelmed her, and then she said faintly:

'I cannot believe it. It cannot be true, that I can be loved like this. It is you that are blind, for I am not like that. You don't know the evil in me, the dreadful things I think sometimes, the shameful things I feel——'

He laughed again, and reached out a hand to brush her cheek.

'Love, beside me you are purity and sweetness itself. And beside almost any woman on this earth. Believe me, for I have known many.'

They were silent then for a long time, gazing into each other's eyes, lost in that depth of emotion beyond words of which he had spoken. Their only awareness was of the other, near and loved, and loving in return. To both of them the impossible, the incredible had happened, and the wonder of it had driven all else from their thoughts.

Shyly, after a little while, she reached up to touch a curl of that shining hair, as if to reassure herself that he was real; and he smiled and imprisoned her hand again in his to take it to his lips. And she longed to feel his arms about her, holding her safe, close, sheltered in the haven she had found at last. But she could see that the builder was standing a little way off, watching them curiously, and she guessed that it was concern for her reputation which kept them apart. She looked him up and down, her mouth spread in a wide foolish delighted smile.

'You are so fine!' she said. 'So you really are Lord Lenoyer?'

'The very same. Nicholas Lenoyer, third Baron of the name.'

'Then this was your home all along?—And it was you,' she went on in a tone of growing wonder, 'who defended the castle when your father was killed and you were only sixteen!'

'How did you hear of that?'

'From Robert—the minister of Pembridge.' One day she would have so much to tell him, but now the questions were crowding to her lips. 'Was that right?'

'Yes.' He nodded. 'That was right.'

'And that is how you know Sir Edward Biddulph—he was a near neighbour of yours. Though you were young to know him well.'

'The acquaintance was forced upon me, to my cost,' he said drily.

'Forced upon you? How?'

'It's a long story——'

'Tell me,' she pleaded.

'Very well,' he agreed. 'You see, we had been hard pressed in that last year of the war, here in the castle. But then the besiegers were called off—they were needed somewhere else, I think—and we had time to renew our supplies and improve our defences. We were only old men and women and children, but we knew we could hold out for many months yet. The only thing we lacked was ammunition.

'And then one day Sir Edward Biddulph appeared at the lake side with a small detachment of soldiers, all well-armed. I knew him only slightly, as a neighbour who had fought with the King early in the war—Did you know that?' Deborah nodded.

'I knew he had come back to his estates after Edgehill, and stayed there quietly ever since. I supposed that, like many another honourable man, his heart was not in the quarrel. So when he stood out there and offered his aid, I believed that his conscience had brought him back to the King's cause, and we let down the drawbridge and opened the gates, and they rode in and we made them welcome.

'And two days later at dusk he opened those same gates to the forces of Parliament.'

'Oh, my dear!' she murmured. 'No wonder you hated him!'

'So that, you see, is why I tried to hurt him when I took you prisoner. I cannot forgive him for the lives that were lost when the castle fell; for what became of this

place that was my home, or for the little blow he struck
so treacherously against the cause I served. And you
know, don't you, why I feel no regret that it happened
to be you I took that night?'

She smiled in answer. He stretched out a hand to
caress her cheek.

'I came back to England expecting to find you
married to him. I rode to Sandwell and they told me he
was wed, and I felt as though the world had fallen to
pieces in my hands; and then I learned her name and I
knew it was not you. I hoped then, against hope, that
you might love me enough to take me. Only to find that
you spurned my hand without even coming to tell me
to my face—if only I'd had the sense to realise it was
not me you spurned, but an unknown suitor. Have
there been so many then, that you've grown uncivil to
them?'

She laughed.

'One after another, ever since the King came back.
And all they ever want is my fortune.'

'Yes, I fear there are many of the King's most loyal
subjects who find themselves the poorer for their
loyalty. You must be generous, dear heart, for surely
you can understand how it is for a man who has given
all to the King's cause to return from years of exile to
find he has no reward but the King's gratitude, and that
his troubles are not over, but often just beginning—But
don't,' he added quickly, 'be so generous as to give your
hand to one of those importunate men!'

'And how do I know,' she asked pertly, 'that you too
are not simply after my money?'

'You wretch!' he said with tender amusement. 'Give
it all to your aunt, and then you will know. I shall carry
you to the altar just the same. Would that satisfy
you?'

'But how then will you rebuild your castle?'

'Ah, I am one of the fortunate ones, my darling. All my lands were confiscated by Parliament, so now I have them restored in full. My days of poverty are over—I do not need a rich wife.'

'Then perhaps,' she teased, 'I should go where I am most needed.'

At that he caught her briefly in his arms.

'Don't, my love. Never say that. My need of you is greater than I can ever say. To live here without you would be like living without the fire in the hearth, the well in the courtyard—there would be no warmth and no refreshment, no purpose to my existence. Believe that, my darling, always.'

'I believe it,' she said gently, 'because I feel it too.'

His lips touched hers lightly, and then he held her from him.

'Tomorrow, when all is settled, I shall kiss you as I ought. Now my builder is waiting and I must go—but first let me show you what I am planning here, and you can tell me if you like it.'

He drew her arm through his and led her to where the other man waited, introducing her by name with great courtesy, and then they all three wandered about the ruins, with the plan for guide, and he pointed out the different rooms he would have, asking for her opinion on the use to be made of them, or the most suitable furnishings. He gave nothing away to their bewildered companion, who was not quite sure where this strange female had sprung from; but their joy and their love vibrated through them, in their voices and her touch on his arm, in their shining eyes and constant laughter.

And then at last Nicholas said: 'If you wait here for a moment, Master Brown, I'll walk to the top of the hill with Mistress Halsey. She ought to be on her way by now.'

They walked slowly over the drawbridge and on up the hill, making each step last for as long as possible, pausing often to gaze into each other's eyes, talking of all that had happened to them.

'I wonder if I shall ever be able to thank you enough for saving my life?' he asked.

'There were thanks enough in the doing of it,' she said. 'For here you are today, because of it——' A dreadful thought occurred to her. 'They won't take you again for it, will they? Someone must recognise you one day, surely?'

'A loyal servant of King Charles condemned under the laws of the Commonwealth is safe enough now,' he reassured her. 'No, it is over now, for good. And what of you? I hope you came to no harm because of what you did.'

Her instinct was to protect him from the truth, to assure him she had not suffered for it. But there must be no secrets between them, now or ever, and she could not hide from him even that small matter.

'I caught a chill, and was in a fever for a few days, but that was all. It was a very little price to pay.'

'I am sorry it took as much as that, my love,' he said. 'I have caused you more fear and hardship than I can bear to think of, when all I want is to love you and care for you and protect you. But when we are married I will try to help you forget the past. You shall have everything I can give you, as well as my love—fine clothes and the most dainty of foods, and gentle horses to ride, and jewels fit for a queen—but only if you want them, of course,' he added with a laugh.

She turned to smile at him; and they walked on in silence to the place where the trees began, and there they halted once more.

'I will come in the morning,' he promised. 'And this time I shall not take no for an answer.'

'You will not need to,' she said impishly.

He bent then and kissed her briefly and gently.

'Until tomorrow,' he said.

Deborah walked back to Pembridge with such a lightness in her heart that it was as if her feet were somehow not quite on the ground. She was dazed with joy, and it filled her being so close to overflowing that now and then she quivered with foolish laughter because she could not help it. If she had met anyone on her way she would not have known, so oblivious was she to anything but her dizzying happiness.

And yet when she entered that gloomy house she almost wondered if it had all been a dream. Out there in the green and blue and gold of the summer day it had all been of a piece, that lovely world and her rejoicing heart. But here nothing had changed. Her uncle's hounds lay by the empty hearth, and one raised his head for a moment as she came in and then settled again to sleep. The dim light, the oppressive quietness, the indefinable odour of cleanliness and unhappy righteousness, were all exactly as they had been before. They even managed to depress her spirits a little.

She had time only to cross to the foot of the stairs before her aunt appeared at the head, full of wrath at her absence, and sent her without delay to help prepare the dinner. Had it been real, that meeting at the castle? she wondered as she made her way to the kitchen. Or was there after all some magic dreamlike quality about the place which for a little space of time could set the world to rights, turn misery to happiness, make the impossible come true; but only while one stood there within the enchanted shelter of the valley? Had she come back now to find that everything was just the same, that she had still to face the problem of her future, friendless and unwanted as she was?

Friendless and unwanted: the phrase rang in her head as she laid plates and tankards on the table. And with it came a sudden chilling recollection. She was friendless and unwanted because she was, in the eyes of the world, a fallen woman, without honour or reputation. It did not matter that it was not through any fault of her own, but that was simply how it was. And Nicholas did not know, for if he had he would surely have spoken of it. Or perhaps, if he had, he would not have come at all to ask her to be his wife.

Her fall had not mattered to those other Royalist suitors; but then they had wanted her fortune, and he did not. And he was quite another kind of man. Would he want her as his wife, the mistress of his beloved home, if he knew the truth?

She shivered, and knew that there was only one thing she could do, cost what it might. When he came tomorrow, joyful, confident, to ask her to be his bride, she must tell him what she was and leave the choice to him. He loved her, but that did not mean he could take her as his wife against what the world would say.

The day dragged appallingly, every trace of happiness gone, leaving only anxiety and a wish that it was all over and she knew the worst. She had been right: it had all been a dream, a wonderful, incredible spell cast by her secret valley to make her deepest wishes take shape for a little while.

She did not sleep very well that night.

It was raining when she woke in the morning, a thorough drenching downpour which obliterated from sight everything beyond the window. She could not even see the garden, still less the woods beyond its walls. She climbed out of bed reluctantly in the early greyness, and dressed without enthusiasm in her everyday grey gown and a clean coif and apron. And then she went down to prayers: her aunt led them now.

Prayers, breakfast in her room, and then she paused for a moment to make sure her hair was out of sight before taking up her empty plate and tankard and moving towards the door.

A sharp knock startled her, and she jumped back a step.

'Come in!' she called, and Betty pushed open the door. The girl looked flustered and anxious, and Deborah put down the things she was carrying so as to be ready with any comfort which might be needed.

'Mistress Deborah,' began Betty, twisting her hands in her apron, 'it's that gentleman again, the one who called yesterday—Lord Lenoyer—he's here again.'

The room swayed about Deborah, and then righted itself. She could feel the colour rising in her face, and she reached out to support herself on the bedpost.

'Please don't be angry—he says he'll not go without seeing you—and Mistress Foster says she'll whip me and you too if you don't come.'

Deborah laid a reassuring hand on the maid's shoulder, her face white now, and said gently: 'Don't be afraid, I'll come.'

But it was she who was afraid as she went slowly downstairs.

Her aunt waited alone in the hall, and came to meet her. 'He's in the parlour. If you dare to refuse him again I'll whip you and then turn you out without a penny. It's more than you deserve, to have this offer twice.'

'Much, much more than I deserve,' thought Deborah, bleakly. 'I was foolish even to think all this could be mine.' She went to the parlour door, opened it, and disappeared into the room, closing the door behind her.

Tall, slender, his fair head brightening the room, his eyes dark with love and tenderness, he stood there:

Captain Black, her highwayman, transformed into Lord Lenoyer, that most eligible of suitors. Yet he was the same man, the only man she had ever loved. She longed to run to him, to pretend everything was as it had been. But she could not do it. If she was not to live always with the guilty knowledge that she had deceived him, with the fear that he might learn the truth by chance, she must tell him.

She reached out her hands to halt his move towards her. He saw the bleakness of her eyes, and dismay transformed his face.

'No, wait,' she said. 'There is something I must tell you.'

And she did so, slowly and haltingly and matter-of-factly, without complaint or recrimination. And when she had finished she stood quite still where she was, and waited. He did not move either, only said softly:

'Deborah, my dear heart, can you ever forgive me for doing that to you?'

She raised her head sharply.

'Oh no, you are not to blame! Please don't think it—— But if you feel that, however much you love me—and I know you do, whatever you may decide—if you feel you cannot have me as your wife, now I am—as I am—then I shall understand. I shall not blame you, and you can go away, and we need never trouble each other again.' She spoke bravely, but the very words were like the slow tolling of a mourning bell.

'Deborah, my love,' he whispered, 'my darling, most generous love. There has never been another woman like you since the world began, and there never will be again. I have known no one, ever, who was so ready to give up everything, love, happiness and all that the rest of us cling to greedily with both hands, because it might be wrong to hold it to her. Your love is deeper and more generous than mine will ever be, though I love you to the depth of my being.

'No, dear heart, if your soul was stained with the blackest crime known to mankind, if you had gone whoring with every man you know, even then I would want you still as my wife—though you would not then be you, my little love, for you are good and sweet and innocent, and no malice could do more than cast a faint shadow on your name—yourself it would never touch. Does that answer you?'

She looked up at him, the colour rosy on her face, the joy slowly, incredibly, returning.

'Yes,' she said softly.

Then in one stride he had crossed the room and swept her into his arms, brushing the coif from her head to let her hair fall in shining glory down her back; and his mouth came down on hers with all the force of his long-restrained passion. And she yielded to it, her body melting into his, her lips parted beneath his kiss, her eyes closed to shut out all but the inexpressible delight and joy of being at last in his arms, her rightful place for ever. The dream was here with her in the room, and it was real, and it would go on and on, and no one now could take it from her.

But for a little while longer they must wait. Slowly, reluctantly, they drew apart, though he held her still in the haven of his arms, looking down at her with grave tenderness.

'You haven't given me your answer,' he said softly.

'You have not asked the question,' she replied.

He held her face between his hands and gazed deep into her eyes.

'It is not your money I want, dear heart,' he said, 'but your life and all you have. You yourself, to be at my side for ever, to share my joys and my sorrows as I will share yours, to complete that part of me that is not whole without you—Deborah Halsey, will you marry me?'